D1527769

AMISH MURDER TOO CLOSE

ETTIE SMITH AMISH MYSTERIES BOOK 4

SAMANTHA PRICE

CHAPTER 1

"Don't they make a lovely couple, Ettie?"

When Ettie took a while to answer, Elsa-May dug her in the ribs.

"Did you say something?" Ettie turned and stared at her sister.

Elsa-May scoffed. "I'm not the one going deaf. I just said, 'Don't you think they make a lovely couple?'"

"*Jah*, they certainly do. A *wunderbaar* couple indeed, and who would have thought it—the girl who was leasing my *grossdaddi haus* and our Jeremiah?"

Jeremiah was Elsa-May's grandson and Ettie's great-nephew.

"*We* thought so, and *that's* why we had them to dinner a few times." Elsa-May couldn't stop a giggle that escaped from her lips, but she froze when the bishop peered at her.

Both Ettie and Elsa-May looked back at the front of the room and remained straight-faced. They knew it was a pet peeve of the bishop that people were rude enough to

1

whisper while he was talking. After a few more words from the bishop, Ava and Jeremiah were pronounced married. They gazed into each other's eyes.

Ettie tilted her head toward Elsa-May, and whispered, "There's nothing like young love."

"It's so long ago, I'm barely able to remember it, but I think I enjoyed it at the time. The glow won't last; after a few years of marriage, the glow wears off."

The two sisters hadn't been that close when they were young wives and both busy with their own families. It was only after their children had grown and their husbands had died that they each sold her farm, and they bought a small house together, rediscovering an adult version of the closeness they'd had as children.

Elsa-May noticed Ettie grimaced, so she quickly added, "Everybody knows that the bloom of new love fades, Ettie, and you can't pretend that your feelings stayed the same after you were married for years."

"I see what you're saying. That warm fuzzy feeling doesn't last, but it's replaced by different feelings as husband and wife grow together."

Elsa-May rolled her eyes. "If that's what you want to say. You're sugar-coating things again."

"I don't think I am. I'm just saying how things are to me."

Everyone around them stood and moved outside Ava's parents' house where the wedding had taken place.

"Come on, we'd better head outside with the rest of them," Elsa-May said in a firm tone.

The elderly ladies walked outside and joined the crowd forming in the yard. Because the weather was fine, the meal after the wedding was to be held in the yard under large spreading trees. Ava and Jeremiah were already sitting down at the wedding table.

"Shall we go over and talk with the happy couple?" Ettie asked.

Glancing over, Elsa-May said, "Let other people talk with them. Let's just sit down here for a moment."

After they sat, Ettie could see through to the kitchen where the women were bustling around preparing the food. "They consider us too old to help with the food these days."

"We've done enough of that in our time, so we are entitled to the rest," Elsa-May said with a wide smile. "I don't mind that the younger women are taking over what we used to do. It suits me to have a rest."

"I guess we've done our part," Ettie agreed.

"In a minute, we'll get up and go and talk with people. I've seen so many people I haven't seen in quite a while."

"*Jah* me too. Seems everyone's come to the wedding."

"I wonder how Brandy will do at the open house," Elsa-May said.

Ettie had decided to sell the home her friend, Agatha, had willed her. Agatha had requested that Ettie allow Ava to stay on in the *grossdaddi haus* as long as she wished. Now that Ava was married to Jeremiah, that left the *grossdaddi haus* vacant, or it would be as soon as Ava moved her things out.

"We'll find out tomorrow unless I call her tonight. She gave me her cell phone number. When the taxi takes us home, we could get the driver to stop at the phone down the road. Then I can phone her. A short walk from the shanty to the *haus* would do us both some good."

"We won't be going home by taxi. I'm certain there will be someone here who can take us home. And besides, that's not a long enough walk. Snowy and I go much further than that two times a day."

Ettie remained silent. Sometimes the best way to deal with Elsa-May's older-sister bossiness was to do just that.

"Anyway, I thought Brandy advised against an open house. Didn't she say people would be turned off that a body was under the *haus* for so long, and an open house would just attract time-wasters?"

"*Jah,* you're right. That's what she said originally, but then she said she'd send emails out to her investors. She's sure one of them will snap the house up, and to make sure one of them did she had them all turn up at the one time to create competition. I think the open house is mainly for the investors."

Elsa-May laughed. "Sounds like something Brandy would do."

"She seems competent at what she does, don't you think?"

"Maybe. I do hope you get some decent money for it. Agatha would have wanted you to get something out of it."

"I miss Agatha."

"We all miss the people who are gone. Ever notice our friends are getting fewer and fewer? Ten years ago it would've been a whole different crowd here."

Ettie looked thoughtful and nodded. "We have to make

friends with younger people. That'll keep us lively and keep our brains ticking over."

"I guess that's what we've had to do. Ava's a good friend of ours now. And I think I have to thank you, Ettie, for getting me Snowy. Now, I've got no excuse not to go for a walk. He does love his walks."

"It wasn't me who got him for you it was Bernie from next door."

"I guess that's right. I'll thank him next time I see him. Bernie didn't get the best welcome when he knocked on our front door with Snowy in his arms. He's a cute dog, but I forgot how much work dogs are." Elsa-May's mouth remained in a thin straight line.

"Snowy's not that much work, and it does give us something to do."

"Getting back to your *haus,* Ettie, I wonder if Ava will be happy living in the *haus* Jeremiah built for them."

"A brand-new house would be a pleasure to live in. He would've built it how she liked it; I'm certain about that. Still, I suppose Ava is a person who gets into the habit of things, and she loved living in the *grossdaddi haus.*"

"And she had her stable right outside and a yard for her horse; everything was right there. I suppose part of the attraction of living near Agatha was independence from her parents. Most girls her age are married," Elsa-May said.

"Jeremiah has made sure everything is perfect. Elsa-May, I've just had a thought, when we leave here let's go past the *haus;* the open house should be just about finished by the time we leave."

"Okay, let's do that. I don't want you to get your hopes

up that the house will get sold quickly. I know Brandy sounds confident, but you have to remember she wasn't enthusiastic about it at the beginning."

Ettie shrugged her shoulders. "It makes no matter to me. With the money Agatha left me it's never cost me a dime to keep it. When I sell it, I'll keep a little aside and divide the rest amongst my *kinner.*"

"Still, it seems Brandy is telling you different things all the time. At one time she's doubtful about getting a sale quickly and another time she isn't. You sure she's not just telling you what you want to hear?"

"We'll soon find out, won't we? She's an experienced realtor; she's been doing it for years and years. From reports I've heard, she has a good reputation."

"She's a sales person, and they tend to tell people what they want to hear. They're trained to do so."

Ettie smiled. "When we get there, someone might be signing a contract."

"We'll soon find out," Elsa-May finally agreed.

"Denke, Elsa-May, that will ease my mind. And if she's already gone by the time we get there, I'll call her later tonight."

Elsa-May nodded.

Ettie looked up to the sky. "When I sold the farm I had my sons to help me with it all."

"They're busy now with their own families. You can't trouble them with simple things you can do for yourself."

"I know; I don't like to bother them."

CHAPTER 2

As the taxi got closer to Ettie's house, she noticed only one car parked outside. "Looks like we've missed Brandy and the open house. I would've expected there to be signs directing people here, and there's only the For Sale sign."

"Nee, she's still here. Isn't that Brandy's car?"

"That's not her car. It's the same color, but a different model. Hers is a new sports car and that one's a sedan."

"I didn't know you knew so much about cars, Ettie. I'd have to take your word for it, then. If it's not her car, then who would have such a fancy car in this neighborhood? And it's parked right outside your *haus.*" Ettie saw horror spread over Elsa-May's face as she rolled down the window, and yelled, "There's someone lying beside the car."

The taxi driver stopped, and the three of them got out of the car and hurried to the woman who lay face down in the gutter.

The driver reached her first. "I know first-aid." He felt for a pulse.

SAMANTHA PRICE

"Is it Brandy?" Elsa-May turned to Ettie.

Ettie couldn't speak and looked on as the taxi driver turned the woman over to feel her neck for a sign of life.

The woman had blonde hair strewn over her face and underneath the hair, her face was a nasty color.

"It's not Brandy, but she looks an awful lot like her."

The taxi driver stated, "No pulse; she's dead. I'll call 911."

While he walked back to his car, Ettie and Elsa-May stood either side of the body staring down at the lifeless woman.

"I wonder what she was doing here," Ettie said.

"You're wondering what she was doing here and not who killed her?"

Ettie remained silent while she stared at the woman. Then she glanced up at her house wondering if the woman had been there. Her gaze darted to a book two paces away closer to the house. After she had hurried to the book, she leaned down, being careful not to destroy any evidence. "Elsa-May, this is an open house list. She must be a realtor. It seems she worked for the same office as Brandy because the papers here have the same company name on them."

"She must be one of Brandy's associates."

"It seems like it. Why don't we call Brandy to see what's going on?" Ettie suggested.

"Good idea. I wonder if she saw anything."

"There's one way to find out. We'll call and see who the woman is, or was."

The taxi driver walked over to them. "I've called 911." He wrote something on a slip of paper and handed it to

8

them. "Here's my number. The police will want to talk with me, but I can't hang around here all day. I've got to make money; I've got five mouths to feed. Tell them to call me if you don't mind."

Elsa-May nodded and looked down at the number now in her hands. "Do you think you might call a realtor for us? Her name is Brandy Winnie. Please tell her what's happened." Elsa-May pointed to the number on the For Sale sign.

"Certainly," he said. "I'll call her from the car."

After he had driven away, Ettie and Elsa-May sat on the steps of the house waiting for the authorities.

"See, this is what happens when you get old, Ettie. The driver didn't think we had anywhere better to be."

Ettie nodded. "That's right; he said he had mouths to feed. What if we had people relying on us to do something or other? When you're old like us, people don't think you've got anybody relying on you. We're supposed to rely on other people."

"*Jah,* you're right."

Ettie looked at the body in front of them. "Such a waste of a young life. I wonder if she had children, a husband or a family. If she wasn't married, she'd most likely have sisters and brothers and other people who'll miss her."

"Did you see those marks on her neck?"

Ettie nodded. "Strangled."

"I thought so too, but I wonder why someone would've done that?"

"Did you see the third finger of her left hand?" Ettie asked.

9

"I noticed. That's where the *Englischers* wear their wedding rings."

"It must be significant that the third finger on her left hand is red and swollen. Someone's pulled her ring off."

"Wedding ring—a token of affection," Elsa-May said.

"I wonder if it was particularly valuable, and she was killed for it? Her car's not that expensive, which leads me to suspect she wasn't that well-off."

Elsa-May gazed at the car. "Looks expensive to me."

"It wouldn't have cost as much as Brandy's car."

Their conversation was drowned out by the sounds of police and ambulance sirens.

Elsa-May stood and pulled on Ettie's arm. "I suppose they'll want to speak with us."

"Well, that's why we've been waiting," Ettie said as she stood.

As they walked towards the road to speak with the police, a dark blue car pulled up behind the police car.

"*Ach nee!* Elsa-May look! It's that Detective Kelly again."

"I thought you two were getting along better. You sound like you don't want to speak with him. Better him than some unknown police officer."

"I suppose, but you can imagine what he will say to us, can't you? Another body here at the *haus;* the same place where Horace was killed. He'll have something smart to say to us about that for sure and for certain."

Ettie's mouth turned down at the corners when she realized how selfish she was being. A woman was dead—most likely murdered, and she was worried about what a detective might say to her.

Elsa-May and Ettie stayed back a little distance as the paramedics and the police gathered around the body. They witnessed Detective Kelly drop to his knees and sob.

Ettie wiped a tear from her eye and whispered to Elsa-May, "I never thought he would have that reaction. Wouldn't he have seen many murders scenes and dead people by now?"

"Maybe he has a heart, Ettie."

Ettie wiped away another tear. Seeing the hardened detective that upset affected her.

The detective glanced over at them, and then rose to his feet wiping his eyes. A few seconds later, he coughed and walked over to them.

"Well, well, well… Ettie and Elsa-May. We meet again, under very similar circumstances." His forehead showed deep furrows as his eyebrows nearly reached his sparse hairline.

These were exactly the sorts of comments Ettie thought that Detective Kelly would make. He'd shrugged off his earlier display of kindness and human warmth.

"Hello, Detective Kelly," Ettie said as Elsa-May nodded to him.

"How was the woman murdered, Detective Kelly, might I ask?" Elsa-May inquired stepping past Ettie.

"Looks like the poor soul's been strangled. She's got marks on her neck; we'll know more once the coroner arrives."

"Was it a robbery?" Elsa-May asked.

"It seems at first look that no money or credit cards were taken. My men will go through the car and ascertain

11

what might be missing. They tell me a taxi driver rang this in."

"We were with him," Elsa-May said as she passed him the slip of paper with the driver's phone number. "He said you could reach him at this number."

He looked at each sister in turn, and then asked, "Did either of you know the deceased?"

Elsa-May answered, "Ettie had an open house here today, and we think she's one of the agents." Elsa-May pointed at the book not far from them that looked as though the dead woman might have dropped it.

The detective looked over at the same time as one of the evidence technicians was picking it up with a gloved hand. He placed it in a bag.

"From what we could read, she's from the same agency as Brandy Winnie, my realtor. Brandy must have left first."

He narrowed his eyes at Ettie. "You didn't touch that book, did you?"

Ettie shook her head. "No, we didn't."

"Never seen the woman before?" he asked firmly.

"No, I'm positive I've never seen her before."

"Me either," Elsa-May added.

"Good. Is there anything else you can think of to tell me?"

"We came here hoping to catch Brandy at the end of the open house. It seems we were too late. The taxi driver said he'd call her," Ettie said.

Elsa-May added, "But then he didn't tell us what she said or whether he called her at all."

"Yes. He was in a hurry to leave."

One of Kelly's men came and whispered something to him, and Kelly looked behind them at the house. When the man left, Kelly said, "We're going to have to look for evidence in your house, Ettie. If you move over this way, we must put tape across it, and you won't be able to go into it until I say it's okay."

As they moved away from the house, the three of them turned when they heard a car come to a screeching halt.

"That's Brandy Winnie now," Ettie said, recognizing her car.

CHAPTER 3

THE TWO ELDERLY sisters and the detective stood and watched Brandy get out of her car. Out of the corner of her eye, Ettie noticed that Detective Kelly stood taller, cleared his throat and straightened his tie. After he'd preened himself, he walked to meet her.

Elsa-May whispered to Ettie, "They're covering the body with a sheet."

Ettie's attention turned to the dead woman. "Let's go back and sit down before we fall down," Ettie said to her sister.

"You can if you want to. I want to hear what Brandy has to say. I'll get a little closer."

Not wanting to be left out of anything, Ettie said, "I'll come with you, then."

Elsa-May and Ettie linked arms and took several steps forward until they were close enough to overhear what the detective said to Brandy. It was Brandy who spoke first.

"Someone called me and said someone is dead. Is it Margo? That's Margo's car there." She was stretching herself to look over to where the body lay.

"I'm afraid the deceased's name is Margo Rivers," he said.

Brandy let out a yell and fell to her knees. The detective kneeled down and put a comforting hand on her shoulder.

Through sobs, she said, "I knew it must've been her when that man called me and described her and her car."

Brandy put her hand to her forehead and sobbed some more.

"Don't worry; we'll get the person who did this to her."

"What happened to her?"

"She was murdered, and that's all we know at this time."

Brandy continued to sob.

"I'll get a female officer," Kelly said.

Ettie thought it must be protocol to get a female officer when a woman needed comforting, although Ettie was certain Detective Kelly would very much like to put his arm around Brandy.

"Come on; we should be with her," Ettie said to Elsa-May

As the elderly sisters walked over to Brandy, she looked up at them. She rose to her feet and wiped her eyes. "Ettie and Elsa-May, were you here too? Did you see anything happen?"

"We came here by taxi and she was on the ground near her car. She had already gone."

"We asked the driver to call you," Elsa-May added.

"We knew you must have known her because she had paperwork with the name of your firm on it."

"Margo's my intern. I had her do the open house instead of me because I was busy with something that came up unexpectedly."

"So, she wasn't supposed to be here?" the detective asked.

Brandy shook her head. "I mean, yes she was. She goes where I tell her to go." Brandy put a hand to her forehead again. "She was newly engaged. Poor Norman will be devastated."

"I'll get his details from you in a minute, but first, when I asked if she was meant to be here, I meant was it a last-minute thing? When did you tell her she was to come here?"

"Only yesterday."

"It was unexpected, but you knew yesterday that you wouldn't be able to attend the open house today?"

Brandy nodded.

The detective retrieved a notebook from an inner coat pocket and scribbled something on it. "We'll need her fiancé's number and the numbers of her next-of-kin."

"You can phone my office for her next-of-kin. They'll have all those details in her personnel file." Brandy pulled her phone out of her pocket to give the detective the office phone number.

"That the phone number there?" he asked pointing to the For Sale sign.

"Oh, yes, of course, that's it. I'll need to give you

Norman's number." Brandy pushed some buttons on her phone.

"You have her fiancé's number in your phone?"

"Yes. He's a client of mine." Brandy read out the number to the detective.

"I'll call this in; I'll be right back." The detective wandered away from them while he made a call.

"I can't believe this is real. It's like a bad nightmare." Brandy sighed loudly.

"I'll need you to come down to the office for questioning, Ms. Winnie." The detective was back already.

"Yes, of course." Brandy nodded.

"Do you know anyone who might have wished Margo harm?" he inquired.

The sisters took a few steps back to be polite.

"No one; no one at all. She was a lovely girl." Brandy gasped. "Do you think someone thought she was me and killed her by accident? Is that why you asked me when I decided to have her come here?"

"Why? Do you have someone who would want you out of the way?"

"I guess I have people who've been angry with me from time to time. There are always clients who miss out on properties for one reason or another. It's always my fault in their opinions."

"What about anything more personal? A jealous boyfriend perhaps?"

Ettie was amused and glanced at Elsa-May who appeared to agree that the last question was an odd one.

"No. I'm too busy for a boyfriend," Brandy replied. "All

I do is work, work, and more work." She smiled at Detective Kelly, and he smiled right back at her.

Ettie stepped forward. "Shall I unlock the *grossdaddi haus,* Detective, so that you can talk with Brandy in more comfort?" Since Ava had already moved out and only had to come and collect furniture, Ettie knew Ava wouldn't mind them going in.

"Thank you, Mrs. Smith, that's very kind. It won't take long then I'll have to inform her nearest and dearest."

"Oh, Ettie, I gave your house keys to Margo," Brandy said. "I don't know where they are now."

"I've got spare keys hidden around the back. I'll get them. I've got one to the *grossdaddi haus* and a spare to the main one." Ettie and Elsa-May headed to the back of the house leaving Brandy and the detective alone.

"Did you hear what was said, Elsa-May? He asked if she had enemies and she said she had a lot."

"Who did? Her or the dead woman?"

"No. Brandy said she—I mean Brandy—has enemies. Remember she told us when she first came to look at the house that she knows many people's secrets? She seems to know a lot about a great deal of people. And not everyone wants their secrets exposed."

"You think someone was trying to kill Brandy?"

"Possibly, if she's the one who was meant to be here. She mailed us a copy of the advertisement that was going into the paper—it was her name on the ad."

"Where are those key?" Elsa-May asked once they were around the back.

Ettie reached under the house and picked up a brick.

19

Under it was a set of keys. Ettie picked it up to show Elsa-May. "There is a key to this house and one to the *gross-daddi haus.*"

After they had unlocked the door of the *grossdaddi haus,* Ettie handed Kelly the key to the main house.

"Thank you, Ettie." He handed the key to one of his men and then the four of them went to where Ava once lived.

Ettie stood at the entrance. "You don't mind us sitting in the living room do you, Detective? We do need somewhere to sit. You might be comfortable if you go through to the kitchen and sit at the table with Brandy."

"Thank you, Mrs. Smith. We shouldn't be too long."

"Take your time, Detective," Ettie said.

Brandy walked through the door followed by the detective. When Brandy and the detective sat in the kitchen, Ettie and Elsa-May sat on the couch in the very next room. The detective got up and closed the kitchen door.

"Shouldn't he be down there with his men to see what they turn up?" Elsa-May whispered.

Ettie gave half a shrug of her shoulders. "I suppose they take it all back to the station and go through the evidence there."

"Sh. Let's see if we can hear what they're saying."

"That's eavesdropping," Ettie hissed.

"Not when the woman was killed on your property; that gives us a right to listen in."

They both heard the detective say, "Do you know anybody who ... do you know anybody ..." he hesitated, and then said, "I'm sorry, I'm distracted by your blue eyes. They're the bluest eyes I've ever seen."

Ettie covered her mouth to stifle a giggle and Elsa-May opened her mouth in shock.

Brandy Winnie's first response was a little giggle, and then she said, "People always tell me that. The funny thing is that there aren't many blue-eyed people in my family."

"Hmm, that is odd, but they're lovely."

"Thank you. Poor Margo, she only just got engaged to a lovely man. Has anyone called him? He'll be devastated."

"I believe you gave me his phone number. I'll get to all the next-of-kin tonight and inform them. What's her fiancé's name?"

"Norman Cartwright."

"*The* Norman Cartwright?"

"Yes. You know him?"

"Everyone around here knows him. He's one of the wealthiest men in the region."

Ettie looked at Elsa-May and pointed to her ring finger. If the man was wealthy, he might have given his fiancée a valuable ring. She had noticed that one of the men on the forensic team had placed paper bags over the woman's hands so they must have considered her hands important. They would surely have noticed her red and swollen finger that was evidence of a missing ring— possibly forced off her finger. Elsa-May nodded to her, acknowledging what Ettie was thinking.

"Margo's life was finally working out well for her. She'd had a rough time, but since she met Norman things had turned completely around for her. He'll be devastated; she was everything to him."

"And what made you swap places with her today?"

"She's my intern and as I already told you I didn't change places with her; I was doing other things, and I had her come here to hold the open. She was to take names and addresses of the people who turned up. It was her duty to take offers and call them through to me."

"We'll take a look at those names; we'll speak to everyone on that list. And did she call you with any offers?"

"No, she didn't. She normally calls me as soon as she gets to her car after an open house. Perhaps she didn't make it to her car?"

"You might be right."

"Do you think someone was angry with her fiancé and then killed her to get at him?"

"That's something we can look into. We'll hear what he's got to say. I'll take your phone number and I will need you to come down to the station tomorrow." After she gave him her number, he asked, "Can I drive you somewhere?"

"No. I've got my car outside."

"Is that a bruise on your face?"

"Yes. I ran into an open cupboard in my kitchen earlier today."

"I don't think you should be driving when you're this upset. Can I phone someone for you?"

"No. I'll be fine. I'll just wait awhile and then drive straight home; it's not that far away. Will you call her parents and call everybody else? I guess that's all under control?"

"Don't worry. I'll do that as soon as I leave here."

The detective and Brandy walked out of the kitchen into the living room.

"Are you two all right?" he asked looking at the two sisters.

Ettie and Elsa-May pushed themselves up off the couch.

"We're okay," Ettie said.

"Just a little weary," Elsa-May added.

Ettie stared at Brandy looking for the bruise that the detective had mentioned. There was a slight mark that Ettie hadn't noticed before.

"Would you like me to drive you home?" Brandy asked them.

"I'll do that," the detective said. "If you ladies don't mind waiting for ten minutes or so?"

"We'll wait," Elsa-May said.

"We're very sorry about your friend," Ettie said to Brandy.

"Thank you, Ettie. I'll be in touch soon."

"You know where we live," Ettie said.

"Yes, I do."

The detective walked Brandy to the door and then had a word with some of his police officers who'd been waiting at the door to speak with him.

When Ettie walked outside, she saw that the body had gone. There was a tow truck attaching chains to the car. She whispered to her sister, "Everything happens so quickly."

"*Jah.* They probably have to take the car in to look for evidence too."

Ettie pressed the lock on the front door handle so it would lock when the door was closed.

"It might be some time before you get the key back for your main house, Ettie. I don't see a problem if you want to go back into the apartment where we just were."

"I understand."

Detective Kelly spoke with some of his men, and after some time he turned and stared at Elsa-May and Ettie with his hands on his hips. When he walked up to them, he said, "I'm ready now. Sorry to keep you waiting."

"Are you sure you can take us home? We can get a taxi."

"You don't live that far. I don't mind driving you."

On the journey to their place, he said, "It's a sad business. The woman was about to get married, and now she's cut down in the prime of her life. I'm determined to get who did this. I'm more determined than I've ever been. I hope you ladies will give me help if I need it."

Ettie pulled her mouth to one side. He'd only ever asked for their help if the case was something to do with the Amish community. "I doubt we'll be able to help you with anything, but let us know."

"Yes, it's dreadful. We were just come back from a wedding ourselves," Elsa-May said.

"Ava's wedding," Ettie added.

"I know Ava; she's the one who lives in the apartment where I was just speaking with Brandy."

"Yes. Ava's moved out now, and we call it a *grossdaddi haus* rather than an apartment. Ava and her new husband are coming to move her belongings out this week."

"I guess there's no use me speaking to Ava if she wasn't there," the detective mumbled.

"No. She was at her wedding. And I don't think she slept there last night either, before her wedding. I'm fairly certain that she slept at her mother's house," Ettie said.

Elsa-May added, "The wedding didn't start until two this afternoon."

CHAPTER 4

WHEN ELSA-MAY PUSHED the front door of their house open, Ettie was close behind her. Snowy rushed at them and danced on his hind legs.

"Back!" Elsa-May said to the small dog, but Snowy didn't listen.

"I see the training's going well," Ettie said with a laugh.

"He's not doing too bad with other things. He's not touched your new slippers yet."

When they walked further into the house, they saw pieces of Ettie's slippers all over the floor.

"What were you just saying?" Ettie asked.

Elsa-May laughed. "I told you to put them up or close your door. He's only a pup."

Ettie leaned down to gather the pieces while Snowy tried to snatch them from her hands. "Do something with him, would you?" Ettie pleaded.

"Snowy, come!"

Snowy immediately walked toward Elsa-May, and then she leaned down and picked him up.

"Did you see that, Ettie? He knows that command. He knows how to come. I'm so pleased with him." She buried her face into his soft fur. *"Gut bu."*

Ettie grunted. "Next time, teach him, 'Don't touch any of Ettie's belongings.'"

"We're still working on that one. It's a work in progress."

"Seems you've taught him not to chew on *your* things," Ettie said as she stood up with pieces of her slippers in her hands.

"He only chews on your things because he likes you. That's how he shows affection."

"Humph. I'd rather get a lick or a wet nose on my leg."

"He's only a pup, Ettie. He'll grow out of the puppy stage soon enough. Another couple years maybe." Elsa-May laughed.

"You should take him for a walk now before it gets dark." Then Ettie murmured, "And to give me some much needed peace and quiet."

"I heard that."

Ettie put the remnants of her slippers in the trash while Elsa-May placed Snowy on the floor and walked toward the door to get his lead.

"Bye, Snowy." Ettie looked forward to the fifteen minutes peace she got every day when Snowy and Elsa-May were out of the house.

"We won't be long," Elsa-May called out before she closed the front door behind them.

"Take your time," Ettie called back. Ettie used to walk with them to get Elsa-May into the swing of it, but now Elsa-May was motivated enough to go alone.

Rather than get the dinner underway, Ettie sat down on the couch and closed her eyes. What harm would it do anyone if the dinner was fifteen minutes later than normal? She tried her best to ignore the horrible feeling gnawing at her over having another dead body near Agatha's house.

She hoped Detective Kelly could find out what happened. In the back of her mind, she knew her house would be even harder to sell when news of the dead woman got out, but worrying wouldn't change what would be.

A loud knock on the front door shattered through Ettie's silence. She knew it wasn't Elsa-May because she would've left the front door unlocked. Ettie opened the door to see Brandy Winnie standing there, looking extremely haggard and not at all like her bright and breezy self. Her bleached blonde hair hung limply about her face, and her makeup from earlier in the day had faded severely.

"Brandy! Come in."

"Thank you." Brandy stepped through the door. "Was that Elsa-May I just saw with a small white dog?"

"Yes, that's Snowy. He needs to be walked often to use up some of his energy. Come and sit down." Once they were on the couch, Ettie said, "How are you feeling?"

"It's been a dreadful shock. It only occurred to me when I got home that you'd be particularly interested in the murdered woman."

Ettie scrunched her nose. "I would be? Why's that?"

"She used to be Amish."

Ettie recalled the dead woman's face. She had

appeared to be in her twenties, late twenties at the most. She hadn't looked familiar in the least, and Ettie knew no one with the first name of Margo. "I don't recall anyone by the name of Margo, and she didn't look like anyone I know. She couldn't have been from around here. Where was she from?"

"Yes she was from here, from your community, I believe. When she came to me a year ago, her name was Margaret Yoder. I advised her to change it so she wouldn't sound so Amish."

"That was Margaret Yoder?" An image of the dead woman flashed in Ettie's mind. "The dead woman had light hair, and Margaret had very dark hair. And Margaret's been gone from the community for over five years."

"She'd been a waitress for years before. I had her bleach her hair and taught her all I knew. Now I'm sorry I ever took her on as an intern."

Ettie raised her eyebrows. "Why did she change her name?"

"She sounded too Amish with that name, Ettie. Margo Rivers sounds snappier. Don't you think so?"

"I like the name Margaret Yoder better."

"Well, I suppose you would, but the Amish aren't our primary clientele."

Ettie wondered if Margaret's parents had been informed about her death.

"Anyway. I thought you should know who she was. I'm sorry, I should've thought to tell you at the house, but I was in such shock that it only came to mind when I got home."

"I'm glad you told me. I do believe her parents have had no contact with her in some time. You said she was to be married?"

Brandy nodded. "I guess he'd know by now. That helpful detective said he was off to let him know."

Elsa-May walked in and unclipped Snowy's lead, and then Snowy scampered straight to Brandy. He pawed at her and clawed her leg.

Brandy stood up after she pushed the dog away. "I don't like dogs; I'm sorry."

"Elsa-May, can you shut him outside, and lock the dog door? Brandy told me something awful; really dreadful."

"What is it?" Elsa-May's eyes grew wide.

"I'll tell you once you've locked Snowy outside."

Elsa-May picked Snowy up and did what Ettie had suggested. She then sat down on her usual chair to find out what was going on. After Ettie had told her the news, she shook her head. "That's awful. I wonder if Detective Kelly has told her family yet."

"I called him on my way here and told him about the name change. I'm sure he would've informed her parents by now. I believe they're quick to tell the families before they find out from the media or in other ways."

Ettie and Elsa-May looked at each other, glad that they wouldn't have to break the news to them.

"We should visit them tomorrow, Elsa-May," Ettie said.

Elsa-May nodded. "Yes, we will. Would you like a nice hot cup of tea, Brandy?"

"I would. I would very much. I'm still in shock." Brandy put her hands to her cheeks. "I feel cold all over."

31

"I'll put the fire on."

"Thank you, Ettie. I have arthritis problems, so the cold makes the pain worse."

"You're too young to have problems like that, surely," Ettie said.

"Unfortunately, it runs in my family. I've had it since I was young. I've had to learn to live with the pain."

"Do you do anything for it?"

"I have an ongoing prescription for strong painkillers."

After Ettie had lighted the fire, she opened a cupboard to retrieve a knitted throw. "Here, put this over you until the fire starts to work."

"Nice. Thank you."

Elsa-May set the tray of tea down on the table and poured the tea.

"I can't work out why you wouldn't have thought to mention when you first met us that a former Amish woman was working for you as an intern," Elsa-May said.

"Margo didn't want it to be known. I knew you'd be at the wedding of your friend, and that's why I had Margo fill in for me. That way, you wouldn't see her and recognize her."

"Margaret has been gone from the community for some time; do you know what she was doing before she became your intern?" Ettie asked.

"I mentioned she was a waitress, but that's not the entire truth, she was a cocktail waitress, and that's how she met her fiancé, Norman. He knew about her past, about the fact she was raised Amish."

"Her fiancé?" Ettie held her head, which was now overflowing with facts. Margaret Yoder had become

Margo Rivers, had dark hair and was a cocktail waitress until she met Brandy, who had tried to turn her into some a Brandy-look-alike realtor.

"Yes. He didn't want to tell people his wife was a cocktail waitress, so he asked me if I'd train her in real estate. He naturally wanted her to learn from the best."

"So, you know Norman well?"

Brandy nodded and looked down. "I took her on. When a man like Norman asks you to do something, you can't refuse him."

"Why's that?" Elsa-May asked.

"He's a very influential man. He's put many deals my way over the last few years, and he's made me a lot of money."

"Would you have lost business, then, when Margaret got her license, or whatever she'd get when you would have fully trained her? I assume an intern means that you were training her?"

"That's right. I was training her, but no, I wouldn't have lost business because I would've kept her under my wing." She looked at Ettie's blank face. "Got a cut out of all her deals," Brandy explained further.

Elsa-May passed a cup to Brandy, one to Ettie, and then settled into her chair with one herself. Brandy took a sip of hot tea and placed the cup back slowly onto the saucer.

"I'm glad you came over to tell us about Margaret. Her parents will be so sad. I'm sure they were hoping she'd return to the community one day. I wonder if they knew she was going to marry soon," Elsa-May said as she reached for a cookie.

"I don't know. She never spoke about her Amish past except to say she had one."

"Who do you think killed her?" Elsa-May got right to the point.

Brandy slowly shook her head. "I honestly can't say. I don't know anyone who'd want her gone. I'm hoping it wasn't a case of mistaken identity, and they meant to kill me."

"You have someone who wants *you* dead?" Ettie asked.

Elsa-May frowned. "You were hoping someone wanted to kill you and not her?"

"No! That would be dreadful; I can't imagine anything worse. And no, Ettie, I don't think I have someone who wants me dead, but would I know if I did? No one has threatened me. I guess one generally doesn't know these things until it's too late."

"And you've discussed your fears with Detective Kelly?" Ettie had overheard her mentioning something along those lines to Kelly.

"I said something to him about it. He wants me to go to the station tomorrow. I suppose he's got more questions." She took another sip of tea. "This is nice tea."

"Thank you," Ettie and Elsa-May said simultaneously.

"It sounds like you got along well with Margaret," Ettie said.

"She was a lovely girl and was liked by everyone. That's why I can't understand a thing like this happening to her."

"Perhaps someone was trying to get at her fiancé? Would he have had enemies? Or does he have enemies that you know of?" Ettie asked.

"He might have, but that's far-fetched and extreme. I mentioned that to the detective. I'm sure he'll look into it. He seems very competent and sure of himself."

"Yes, he is," Ettie said nibbling on a cookie she'd just taken off the plate near the teapot.

"Is he married?" Brandy asked blinking rapidly.

Ettie studied Brandy's face. Surely she couldn't be interested in the detective. "Who? Detective Kelly?"

Brandy nodded.

"No. He's not married," Elsa-May said.

Brandy couldn't hide the smile that turned her lips slightly upward at the corners.

"It must be hard with a job like his. The old detective that he replaced isn't married either. He said he was married to the job." Ettie gave a little laugh.

"He's retired now, though. I thought he had a thing for Myra once, Ettie."

"Nothing ever came of it. Myra's my daughter," Ettie explained to Brandy.

"Who had a thing for your daughter, Ettie? Are you still talking about Detective Kelly?"

Ettie laughed. "No, we're talking about our old detective, Detective Crowley."

"I see." Brandy took another sip of tea.

"Do you have someone who can stay with you tonight, Brandy?" Elsa-May asked.

"No, why? Do you think I'm in danger?" Brandy drew her fingers down the length of her hair that hung over her shoulder.

"No, not at all. I thought you might appreciate staying with a friend, or having one stay with you."

SAMANTHA PRICE

Brandy pushed her hair behind her back then flicked her head. "I'm a loner; I don't have close friends. There have been many tough times, and I'll get through this one too."

"Were you close to Margaret?"

"It's so strange to hear you call her Margaret. She was always Margo to me. She was my intern, but I wouldn't call her a friend. Were we close? I suppose that's subjective." Brandy gasped and then set her tea down on the table.

"What is it?" Ettie asked.

"I just thought of someone who might want her out of the way."

"Who?" Ettie and Elsa-May asked simultaneously.

"Norman has a daughter, Paisley, and she was his sole heir, but if Norman had gotten married, she'd most likely have her inheritance split down the middle, or worse."

"You think she might have killed to protect her inheritance?" Elsa-May asked.

"But why outside my house? And would a woman have the strength to strangle her?" Ettie inquired.

"It was just a thought. She could've paid someone to do it. Her father gives her quite an allowance. Paisley wouldn't be the type to get her hands dirty."

"It would definitely be worth mentioning those things to the detective when you see him tomorrow, Brandy."

"Thanks, Ettie. I don't know why I didn't tell him today, but I will mention it to him." Brandy finished her last mouthful of tea. "And this all happened near your house, Ettie. It's not good for the value to have another murder there. Do you realize it will affect the price?"

"Can't be helped. God has it in hand." Ettie smiled at Brandy hoping she would calm down a little.

Brandy looked surprised when Ettie spoke about God. "I'm sure He has things in hand. Well, I should go." She folded the blanket, stood, and placed her teacup on the table in front of her. "Thank you for the tea, and I'll be speaking to you both soon. Maybe we should give things at the house a rest, Ettie?"

"That would be a good idea, Brandy. I'll leave it in your capable hands."

Ettie and Elsa-May both walked Brandy to the door, and then they stood in the doorway watching her drive away in her sleek black car.

"Now that's a sports car," Ettie said to Elsa-May, to which Elsa-May nodded.

"I never would have guessed that the dead woman was Margaret. She really looked nothing like herself; nothing like her at all."

"We hadn't seen her for years, though, Elsa-May."

Elsa-May walked to the back of the house and unlocked the dog door. Snowy came bounding through as though he'd been sitting right there waiting for it to be unlocked.

"He's got so much energy for a dog that's just been for a walk," Ettie groaned as she watched him.

"I had to cut the walk short when I saw Brandy drive past," Elsa-May said.

"I'll peel the vegetables for dinner."

"I'll help."

As the sisters sat down at the table to peel the vegetables, Ettie said, "You know, I remember that Margaret was nearly married and then she stopped the wedding just days before it was to happen. Do you remember that?"

"That's right. She was to marry Josh Tomson. I'd forgotten all about that. He was devastated and didn't leave his parents' *haus* for months. Some say he had a breakdown."

"And that's why he's remained single to this day. Maybe he'd been so in love with Margaret that he could never look at another woman," Ettie suggested.

"Or so betrayed by her, he could never trust himself to love another woman again."

Ettie placed her knife down and leaned back in her chair. "Either way, I wonder if Kelly might see him as a suspect."

"He very well could, but I doubt Josh would turn to murder."

"Nee, he wouldn't." Ettie shook her head.

"Shall we visit Margaret's parents tomorrow?"

Ettie pulled her mouth to one side. "I think we should leave it another day to give Detective Kelly time enough to see them."

"Jah, you're right. We don't want to be the ones to break the news to them."

"Don't forget we have to visit Detective Kelly tomorrow."

"I wonder what he'll ask us. I hope he's found out something."

CHAPTER 5

THE NEXT DAY at Ettie and Elsa-May's visit to the station, Detective Kelly had only ten minutes to speak with them.

"This way."

The followed him to his office, and when they sat down opposite the detective, Ettie said, "I suppose you already know the dead woman's real name was Margaret Yoder?"

"Yes, we do. How and when did you find that out?" The detective slumped into his chair.

"Brandy came to our house last night."

Elsa-May nodded. "Yes, she thought we'd be interested to know."

"Did you already know that, Detective?" Ettie asked.

"How could I have known something like that right away? I looked into things and found it out." The detective appeared to be annoyed; he picked up his take-out coffee and took a mouthful.

"It's just strange that you asked, or mentioned that you might need our help before you knew the woman was

Amish." Ettie turned to Elsa-May. "Do you remember him saying something like that?"

"Yes, but he only said that in relation to the fact that the body was found on your property, Ettie."

"Okay," Ettie said. "That seems reasonable."

The detective said, "Elsa-May's quite right. How would I have known the woman was raised Amish? She certainly wasn't dressed Amish, and there was no sign on her forehead."

Ettie frowned and breathed out heavily at the detective's sarcasm.

"What questions do you have for us?" Elsa-May asked.

"I'm afraid I have none today; maybe tomorrow. The autopsy report isn't back yet, and neither are the forensic results. Some of the results might not be back for weeks. I should have some later today, though."

"Have you spoken to Margaret's family already?"

He gave a sharp nod. "I informed them yesterday."

"That must have been dreadful news for them."

"We were going to visit them. We might leave it for a day or two, Ettie."

"I think that's best," Ettie responded.

The detective stood. "I've no more questions for the moment. You should have access to your house soon, Mrs. Smith. I'll personally bring the key back to you when the team is finished with it."

"We'd appreciate that, Detective," Ettie said.

"And I will have more questions for you as more information comes to light."

TWO DAYS LATER, Elsa-May and Ettie visited Margaret's parents. Margaret was the youngest of seven children and the only one who'd left the community.

When they knocked on the door, Margaret's mother, Rose, opened it. "Nice to see both of you. Come inside."

Rose certainly didn't look as though she'd lost a child.

"I've had a few visitors. I suppose you've heard about Margaret?"

"Yes, we have. Elsa-May and I were the ones who found her. She was working as a realtor and doing an open house on Agatha's old *haus* that I decided to sell."

"I wasn't told about that part, but I didn't ask too many questions of the men who came here," Rose said her bottom lip quivering.

Rose turned and walked into her living room, and the two sisters followed. When Rose sat down, so did Elsa-May and Ettie.

"I had detectives come and tell me she was found murdered." A tear came to the corner of her eye, and she wiped it away and lifted her chin.

"We're both sorry for your loss, Rose."

"Don't be. She made her choices, and those choices had nothing to do with the way she was raised. I can't make any of my *kinner* or my *grosskinner* stay on the narrow path. It's a choice they have to make on their own. *Strait is the gate and narrow's the way.*"

"When will the funeral be?" Ettie asked.

"I'm having nothing to do with that. The detective told me she was to be married to an *Englischer,* and I'm going to let that man take care of things."

"Will you go?" Elsa-May asked.

"Nee. I'll not go to an *Englischer's* funeral, and that's what she was." She stared at the elderly sisters' faces. "Don't look so shocked. I did everything for her when she was alive. *Let the dead bury their own dead."*

Ettie had never heard Rose be so bluntly. Perhaps that was her way of coping with the loss of a child. Not only had Margaret died, but she'd also died as an *Englischer* and Amish beliefs were that she would never enter the kingdom of God. Her soul was lost for eternity.

Elsa-May asked Rose, "Do you ever hear from Josh Tomson? I know he used to spend a lot of time at your *haus* many years ago when Josh and Margaret were courting."

Rose shook her head. "That was another disappointment she gave us. That poor man; he never got over her leaving him. I don't know how he would've taken the news that she was going to marry someone else. She ruined his life completely. I won't allow her to ruin mine. I've got other *kinner* and *grosskinner* to care for."

"As you said, Rose, everyone has to make their own choices. Margaret did just that. She lived as an *Englischer,* but does that mean you shouldn't go to her funeral?" Elsa-May asked. "You might feel better after a final goodbye."

Rose tilted her chin high. "I will not go."

"Perhaps you might regret that decision later on?" Ettie added.

She shook her head emphatically. "My mind's made up, and Gideon agrees with me."

Ettie wasn't surprised that Rose's husband, Gideon, thought that way. He was the kind of person who saw everything in black or white.

"Is there anything we can do for you?" Elsa-May asked.

"Nee. We're fine. She was dead to us long ago. I can't say the same about Josh, though."

Ettie studied Rose's face to get a clue what she meant by her last comment. "You think Josh was still in love with her after all these years?"

"He's a shadow of the person he used to be before she shamed him."

"Josh was a lot older than Margaret, wasn't he?"

"Yes, he had a good ten years on her."

Ettie wasn't quite sure what Rose meant about being 'a shadow of the person he used to be.' He had gained many pounds, so he certainly had not wasted away to become a shadow in that sense.

"And do you mind if I ask how old Margaret would've been?" Elsa-May asked.

"Twenty-six. She had the same birthday as Russell, her *bruder,* and he was four years older. He just had his thirtieth birthday."

After Ettie got 'the look' from Elsa-May that she was ready to go, she said, "Let us know if you need anything. We've got people we need to see in town."

"Are you sure? Why don't you stay and I'll put a pot of *kaffe* on?"

"Nee, we've got appointments and errands to run. *Denke,* anyway," Elsa-May said. "Can you possibly call us a taxi?"

"Of course." Rose went into the barn and called them a taxi. When she came out, she waited with them on the porch until the taxi appeared.

As soon as they were driving away, Elsa-May asked, "Well, what did you think of that, Ettie?"

"A little bit of a surprise."

"Which part?"

Ettie pulled a face. "All of it really. I can't understand people who can wipe their *kinner* from their memory just like that. *Gott* gives everyone a choice in what they believe. Is it right or even fair to block their hearts when someone does not believe the same thing they do?"

"It's easier for them that way. If they don't think about them, they don't go through any pain. Also by turning their backs, they hope it will bring their *kinner* home to them."

Ettie nodded. "I suppose that's true about being easier, but I've never been able to believe that if someone turns their back or disowns their *kinner*, it will cause them to return. I've never seen that be the case. If it were me, it would give me more reason to stay away."

"I don't agree, Ettie. They're doing it for the *gut* of their *kinner*."

"Each to their own way of thinking."

"That's why we have shunning. I suppose you don't believe in that?"

Ettie shrugged. "It's not for me to say."

"I can see Rose's point. Grieving won't bring Margaret back, but it will make her feel worse if they fret and go through all the things they could've done differently. When in fact, nothing would've changed. I can see why Rose is hardening her heart."

"Should we just go home, then? I don't want to get caught up in another murder investigation. Let's leave

Detective Kelly to handle this one. This one's too close to home. Especially when I've got Myra who's still out of the community." Ettie wiped a tear from her eye. "I pray for her daily."

Elsa-May nodded, which was just as well because Ettie had already given the taxi driver their home address and they weren't far away.

CHAPTER 6

THEY HADN'T BEEN HOME LONG when a knock sounded on Ettie and Elsa-May's front door.

"Who could that be?" Ettie asked as she pushed herself up from the couch.

They only had one couch in their small living room. The rest of the room was filled with old wooden chairs and one coffee table. Elsa-May was happy to sit and knit for hours in one of the chairs.

"It could be Brandy again," Elsa-May said.

Ettie opened the door to see Detective Kelly.

She smiled at him. "Come in. I've been wondering what you've been able to find out."

He handed Ettie her key. "Thank you. You're free to go back to your house."

"Good."

The detective walked a few steps and sat down in their small living room on one of their rickety chairs. After he nodded hello to Elsa-May, he said, "Did you visit Margaret's parents?"

"Yes, we saw Rose, her mother, this morning."

"We didn't even recognize Margaret, but we didn't tell her mother how much she'd changed."

"How well did you know Margaret?" Kelly asked.

Before Ettie could answer, Elsa-May said, "Brandy told us she'd changed her name and dyed her hair. Her name was Margaret Yoder, and Brandy told her to change it to Margo Rivers."

"Yes, we know all of that, but I do find it rather odd and perplexing that neither of you recognized the woman as coming from your own community."

Elsa-May frowned. "She looked completely different. We hadn't seen her for a good five years and back then she had dark hair and was dressed very differently."

"Significantly different, and she was wearing makeup, which we don't wear at all," Ettie added.

"Yes, makeup can change a woman's looks drastically," Elsa-May said.

"I suppose that's true," the detective agreed.

"How did she die? Was she strangled?" Ettie asked.

He nodded. "Yes, that's how she died. I also requested a complete toxicology screen, but that will take weeks to come back. That's just in case she had anything in her system."

"You think she might have been poisoned as well?"

"I just want all bases covered. Ettie, in my investigations I've come across a name."

Ettie looked at him hoping he wouldn't say, Josh Tomson.

"That name is Josh Tomson. Do you ladies know him?"

"We do. He and Margaret were going to be married,

but at the last minute, she called a halt to everything and that's when she left our community. Well, very soon after."

"Could he possibly be harboring a grudge of sorts?" The detective leaned forward and stared from one sister to the other.

"I think he was understandably upset, Detective, but I don't know if he would've held a grudge," Elsa-May stated.

"I tried to talk with him and couldn't get anything out of him. Essentially, he refused to comment. Could you possibly find out for me, Mrs. Smith?"

Ettie's mouth turned down at the corners. "I don't know him that well. What am I supposed to ask him?"

"Find out how he's taken the news of her death." He agitatedly scratched his chin. "I believe Josh is heavily involved in her murder."

"No! He would never be," Ettie blurted out.

"How have you come to that conclusion?" Elsa-May asked.

"I have to keep that to myself, but I do need your help again, Mrs. Smith."

Ettie pulled a face. "I will help, but only to prove you wrong about Josh."

"Fair enough. I want you to find out what he knows. See if he was close with Margo or had any contact with her recently, and if he did, find out what she said to him."

"If he's involved like you think, why would he tell us anything?" Ettie asked.

"You just have to trust me. I can tell you more later, not now. I'd like you to find out what you can from him

49

before I interview him again. Or, I should say *try* to have another talk with him."

Ettie looked over at Elsa-May. "Will you come with me?"

"If I have to," she replied.

"Good. I suppose we'll go tomorrow, Detective." She looked back at her sister. "I don't even know if he still lives with his parents or not."

"He doesn't. He lives with Arthur Gosling," Elsa-May said.

"Does he?" Ettie raised her eyebrows at him living with the older Arthur Gosling. She wondered what the two would have in common. "How do you know that and I don't?"

"It is surprising; it's a wonder you don't know. They've been sharing old William Harrington's house for a good two years. It makes sense to share a house and split the expenses since they both look like they're never going to marry."

"I suppose that's true if Josh doesn't want to stay with his parents. In my day, no one moved out of their parents' home; if they didn't marry, they just stayed on."

"Thank you, both of you, I'd appreciate anything you can find out. I need to ask the right questions when I visit him, and that's why it's so important you find out what you can."

"Do you have any suspects other than the misguided notion that Josh Tomson is involved?" Elsa-May asked.

He raised his brows. "We're following up on a few leads."

Ettie could tell by the detective's tight-lipped response

that he didn't want to share what those leads were. She thought she'd give him a little prod especially since he had asked for her help. "Brandy mentioned that Margaret was engaged to someone, and we did notice that the third finger on her left hand was swollen and red."

He nodded. "I suppose I can let you in on this much; her engagement ring is missing. It was a large diamond. Margo's fiancé, Norman Cartwright, claims the ring was set with a single diamond of eight carats and of extremely pure quality."

Elsa-May pulled a face. "Strange he'd admit to a thing like that. I thought a man with his wealth would give the woman he was about to marry something good."

"It is good, Elsa-May. That's what the detective just said."

Elsa-May scrunched up her nose and looked at the detective. "You said the diamond was poor quality."

Ettie giggled and covered her mouth. "I keep telling you your hearing's going. No, Elsa-May, he said the ring was an eight carat diamond of *pure* quality, not *poor* quality."

Elsa-May laughed. "I see, so a large good diamond, then, Detective?"

"To be exact, the paperwork says it's a D which is the best color a diamond can be, which is actually no color at all. It does have a few white spots within the stone that can't be seen without magnification. According to the paperwork Cartwright provided us with, it did have a laser-inscribed number on its girdle. The girdle is the perimeter of the stone. Cartwright didn't want to talk about the diamond; he said he'd deal with the insurance claim later. It's hard to deliver bad news to people who are so in love."

"You delivered the news to him yourself?" Ettie asked.

He nodded. "I did. In murder cases, I like to be there to see people's reactions."

"And what was his reaction?" Elsa-May asked.

"Inconsolable was what he was. He's a broken man."

Ettie said, "Brandy says that he has a daughter."

"She wasn't home at the time. I've got her coming into the station tomorrow as soon as she gets back from a business trip. I suppose Brandy also told you that the daughter would have been disadvantaged in her father's will if he'd married Margaret?"

Ettie nodded. "She did mention something along those lines. We visited Margaret's mother, and she said her family was having nothing to do with the funeral. We were wondering whether Norman is organizing that?" Ettie asked.

The detective appeared not to be listening to Ettie. "As you know, the night of the murder, I went to visit Margo's, or I should say, Margaret's family. I called her Margaret while I was there. They're not happy that she had changed her name. Anyway, they were polite, but they were restrained."

"I guess that's just how they are," Elsa-May said. "It would be hard to hear something like that. They'd already cut her off in their minds and their hearts since she left all those years ago and that's possibly the only way they can cope. And you brought news that killed any hope they had of her coming back to the community."

"I'm sorry, Ettie, you asked me about the funeral?" the detective asked.

"I did. Do you know who's organizing it? Rose, Margaret's mother, said that they weren't organizing anything."

"As far as I know, her body hasn't been released yet. That might happen later today. If Margaret's parents don't want to handle the arrangements, I'd guess that Norman would be happy to do that. Do you plan on going to the funeral yourselves?"

"Yes, we'd like to go and pay our respects," Ettie said.

"I'll let you know when I find out what the arrangements are."

"Thank you. We'll visit Josh tomorrow and then we'll drop by the station and let you know what we've found out." Ettie heaved a sigh.

The detective looked at Snowy sleeping in his bed in the corner. "Still haven't found a taker for that dog yet, Elsa-May?"

"No. She wants to keep him now," Ettie said firmly before Elsa-May could say anything. "He's part of the family now."

"He certainly looks like he's made himself at home." The detective stood. "I can expect you ladies at the station after you've talked with Josh Tomson?"

"Yes, that's right. He might be hard to track down, but we'll see you afterward. He'll be at the Sunday meeting, so we might have to wait until then." Elsa-May rose to her feet.

Ettie and Elsa-May showed the detective to the door.

"Thank you for your fingerprints and giving us your DNA for elimination purposes, ladies."

"I'm certain you already would've had all that on record, but we're always happy to comply."

"Have you found something else out that you're keeping to yourself?" Ettie asked.

"We did, but that's all I can say at the moment. I've got the taxi driver coming in and Norman Cartwright, his daughter, and Josh Tomson. I'm hoping they'll all submit to DNA testing. We need samples from all of them. Well, good day, ladies."

When the detective left, Snowy woke up and sniffed where the detective had been.

"Not much of a watchdog, are you Snowy?" Elsa-May said as she sat down again.

Ettie leaned down and picked Snowy up and then sat on the couch with him on her lap. "That's going to be awkward, Elsa-May. We can't turn up where Josh's living and start asking him questions. He'll know we're asking because Margaret's been found dead. And he'll wonder what business it is of ours to be asking him anything."

Elsa-May thought for a moment and then said, "I can't think of a reasonable excuse for talking with him either."

"It's Friday now and this Sunday there's a meeting on, so that's only a couple of days to wait. That will seem more natural."

"I would feel more comfortable with that, but now we have to come up with something to ask Josh. And find a way to bring Margaret up in the conversation," Elsa-May said.

"I could mention something about her being found just in front of Agatha's *haus.*"

"*Jah* say something like that. Anyway, I'll stay close so I can back you up if you stumble over words or forget what you're saying."

"*Denke*, Elsa-May, that'll be good. I know I'll be nervous speaking with him. I don't know what the detective thinks Josh has to gain. Brandy has obviously got this all wrong; she's mistaken somehow."

Elsa-May chortled. "Why can't we live a peaceful life? Seems like something is always happening."

"I had hoped we could keep out of the whole thing, but it's not easy when the woman was found dead after doing an open house for me at my *haus.*"

"The detective never mentioned if he'd followed up all the people from the open house. He might find some leads there; someone might have seen something."

"Perhaps we could find out next time we see him. It makes me feel uneasy that the murderer might have been in the *haus.*"

"I wonder what other leads the detective is following up."

CHAPTER 7

WHEN THE SUNDAY meeting was over, Ettie and Elsa-May moved outside the Shrocks' house amongst the crowd. Ettie had her eyes on Josh, and if they stayed close to him, she hoped they could strike up a conversation.

Just as Ettie was staring at him, he looked over and caught her eye. Then, he walked toward them.

"Hello, Josh."

"Hi, Ettie, Elsa-May."

Elsa-May nodded, and then he cleared his throat as though he was about to say something.

"Ettie, I heard that Margaret was found outside your *haus?* Can I ask you about it?"

Ettie stepped closer to him. "Of course, you can."

He looked down at the ground, licked his lips, and then looked up at her. "Do you think she suffered?"

"I really don't know. The police say she was strangled, and she did have marks on her neck."

"You saw her?"

"Jah, both Elsa-May and I saw her. She had just

57

finished an open house for me, and as we drove up in the taxi, we saw her lying there." His face contorted, and Ettie thought he might cry. "I'm sorry, Josh, I don't know how much you want to know."

He looked up and blinked hard. "I can't believe she's gone. It doesn't seem real."

"When did you see her last?" Elsa-May asked.

"Not since she left. I'd hear about her, though. People would tell me things about her and the man she was to marry."

"You heard she was engaged?"

He nodded. "I did."

"What did people tell you about him, if I can ask you that?" Ettie said.

"I heard he wasn't a reputable person. Well, there's not a polite way to say it. He was dishonest was what I heard."

Ettie blinked hard. "Dishonest? In what way?"

"I'm not certain, but I heard he was in some shady deals. I didn't really listen too much. Now I wish I had taken more notice."

"Do you remember who told you these things?" Elsa-May asked.

He shook his head. "Can't say that I do."

Ettie bit the inside of her lip. What was it that the detective wanted her to find out? She found out he hadn't seen her since she left, and he'd heard things about her fiancé being involved in dishonest dealings. They hadn't really found out anything useful for the detective at all. "Do you know anyone who might have wished her harm?"

He shrugged his shoulders. "I wouldn't know. As I said, I haven't seen her in years."

Elsa-May patted him on his shoulder. "We know it's upsetting for you."

"Denke. I'll just have to get used to her being gone. You know, I always thought she'd come back. That had been in my hopes and prayers every day."

The man looked genuinely upset, and Ettie was certain he was innocent. A man who had been hoping and praying that a woman would come back to him didn't sound like the same kind of man who would have been unkind.

He looked to his left. "I might say a word to her parents. Excuse me." Josh left the ladies alone.

Ettie turned to look at Elsa-May. "What do you make of that?"

"He certainly seemed genuinely upset."

"And he hasn't seen her for years."

"I wonder what exactly he heard about Margaret's fiancé?" Elsa-May asked.

"It could be just rumors. Wealthy people are often surrounded by rumors. People do like to create drama; maybe that's all it was. There might have been no truth in it at all."

"I know the detective's wrong about him being involved. How could he have anything to do with her death?"

"That might be true. Look, there's Ava." Ettie pointed over to where Ava was.

They waved to Ava, and she came over to them.

"Hello! I'm an old married lady now." She giggled.

"About time too," Ettie said with a smile.

The happiness quickly left Ava's face. "Ettie, I heard

59

that Margaret Yoder has been murdered and found outside our *haus*."

"*Jah*, that's true. We drove there in a taxi to see how the open house went. We expected to see Brandy, but instead, Margaret was there lying on the ground near her car."

Elsa-May was quick to point out, "We didn't know it was her. She'd changed a lot. She'd even changed her name and her hair was light."

Ava put her fingertips to her mouth. "Hasn't Josh Tomson been waiting for her to come back to him? That's what I've heard."

Ettie nodded. "*Jah*, he's very upset. We were just speaking to him."

"Who do they think killed her? Do they have any idea?" Ava asked quietly.

Ettie shook her head. "None at this stage. None at all."

"She was to be married," Elsa-May said. "The detective said the man she was going to marry was very rich. What was his name again, Ettie?"

"Norman Cartwright."

"That's right."

"Brandy Winnie tells us that Norman's daughter wasn't too happy about sharing her inheritance when her father married Margaret."

"Isn't that a motive?" Ava asked.

Ettie pulled her mouth to one side. "I suppose we'll just wait to see what the detective uncovers."

Ava's eyes grew wide. "Detective Kelly?"

The elderly sisters nodded.

"Has he asked for your help again, Ettie?"

"He asked me to talk with Josh to see what I could find out. Then he's going to speak with him."

"Did Josh tell you anything when he was speaking to you just now?" Ava asked.

"Nee. He said he hasn't seen her in years."

Elsa-May added, "But he did say that he heard about her intending to marry, and that the man wasn't always honest in his dealings. Ettie thinks it's just a rumor."

"Well, it'd be hard to know, wouldn't it?" Ava blurted out, "Wait a minute. Did you just say that he said he hadn't seen her in years?"

Ettie nodded. "That's what he said."

"That's not what I heard. I happen to know that Josh met with Margaret regularly, and that's why Josh found it hard to let her go."

"Do you remember who told you that?" Elsa-May asked.

"Jeremiah told me. He's good friends with Josh."

Ettie and Elsa-May stared at each other, both wondering why he'd lie about that.

"Do you want me to try to find anything out?" Ava asked.

Ettie shook her head. *"Nee denke,* Ava. You go and enjoy married life and settling into your new home."

"Jeremiah and I will be over at the *haus* tomorrow to collect all my things. And then we'll give the place a final clean."

"Denke, Ava, but I don't know if there's any hurry to move your things now. The place is going to be that much harder to sell now, with Horace's body being found under

the floorboards some time ago, and now this happening with Margaret out in front of the house."

"I didn't think of that. Sorry to hear that, Ettie. It's such a nice *haus.*"

"I know, but I can't worry about that. It'll sell when it sells."

"We'll still get all my furniture out and clean it tomorrow. I don't have a lot to move."

Ettie nodded. "The police might still have the main *haus* taped up so don't go near that one. Well, maybe not since he gave me back the key."

"I won't go near it."

When Ava went off to talk to other people, Ettie whispered to Elsa-May, "If Josh wasn't telling the truth about not seeing Margaret for years, he probably wasn't telling the truth about Norman Cartwright being dishonest."

"It might make him feel better to believe bad things about the man he lost Margaret to. Should we speak with Brandy again?"

"Perhaps. She certainly seems to know what's going on." Ettie noticed Margaret's older sister had walked up to them. "Hello, Sarah," Ettie said.

She smiled and nodded politely to both elderly sisters. "My *mudder* told me that you were the ones who found Margaret."

"We were."

"She hadn't even kept in contact with us. My parents are upset, but they'd never let it show. Do you know when there will be a funeral? I'd like to go."

"We've been waiting to find out too. The detective is going to let us know; we'll tell you as soon as we find out."

"You can come with us," Elsa-May offered.

"*Denke,* I'd like that. You've got my phone number haven't you?"

"We don't, but we have your *mudder's.*"

"I'd rather you not tell anyone I'm going to the funeral. It would only make everyone upset. I'll find someone to look after my three young ones. I know Margaret hadn't always done the right thing, but she was still my little *schweschder.* I'll find paper and pen and give you my number before you leave."

Ettie and Elsa-May agreed, and then Sarah hurried away just as their great-grandchildren spotted Ettie and Elsa-May. Three young boys and two girls came bounding up to them.

"Can I come and stay with you again, *Mammi?*" six-year-old Ivy asked Elsa-May.

Elsa-May put a hand on her shoulder. "You can soon, if it's all right with your *mamm* and *dat.*"

"I'll go see."

Just before she ran away, Elsa-May added, "Not today. I said soon."

Ivy was the only one who had ever stayed at their house on an overnight visit. The others wanted to stay close to their parents.

Elsa-May watched Ivy running to her parents. "She reminds me so much of myself."

Bossy? Ettie thought to herself between talking to the remaining great-grandchildren.

A few moments later, Ivy came bounding back. "They said they'll talk with you about it, *Mammi.* I think they'll let me."

"Gut, Ivy. It'll be nice to have you over again soon."

"Do you know *Mammi's* got a dog now?" Ettie asked Ivy.

"You have?"

Elsa-May nodded. "And I'm certain he'd like to play with you."

"We've got dogs too," Ivy said.

"This one is small. He's about your size."

"As big as me?"

Elsa-May laughed. "Not as tall, he's the right size for you to play with. He's about this high." With her hands, Elsa-May showed her how big Snowy was.

A look of delight spread across Ivy's chubby face.

When the children went to speak to someone else, Ettie said, "It's most likely not a good time to have her to the *haus* with all the murder things happening."

"I know, but I find it hard to say no to her when she looks up at me with those big blue eyes."

"You'll have to put her visit off until this whole thing's wrapped up. I wouldn't want her there when Detective Kelly comes to the house."

"I know. He might scare her."

"He scares us sometimes."

"I'll let her parents know that she can come in a few weeks time."

"Hopefully, this whole thing will have settled by then, and Detective Kelly will have found the killer."

CHAPTER 8

THE FOUR LADIES went to the funeral of Margaret Yoder although she was being buried as Margo Rivers since her name had been legally changed. In the taxi with the elderly sisters was Ava, and Margaret's older sister, Sarah.

Ettie kept quiet, feeling she couldn't speak freely with Sarah in the car. She didn't know what might upset her. She certainly didn't want Sarah to know that the detective had asked her to find something out from Josh Tomson.

Norman Cartwright had arranged the funeral.

They pulled up right outside a handsome white church, which was dwarfed by the large trees that surrounded it.

"Just let us out here, thank you," Elsa-May said to the driver.

The ladies got out of the taxi, and after Ettie had paid the driver, she joined them on the sidewalk. There was a crowd of people gathered outside the church, and just as the ladies approached, everyone began to move inside.

They took a row of seats at the back of the church. A

raised platform at the front was mostly covered with tall vases of roses. The white coffin in the center covered with pink roses took prime place. Beside it, a large photograph of Margaret sat on a white easel.

"That looks nothing like her." Tears fell down Sarah's face when her eyes fell on the photo.

Since Ettie was sitting next to her, she patted her on her arm.

"I can't go through this. I thought I could, but *Mamm* was right. I shouldn't have come. I'll wait outside." Sarah stood, moved past Ettie, and walked outside.

"What's wrong with her?" Elsa-May, who was sitting on the other end of the row, leaned across Ava, to ask Ettie the question.

"She's just upset. She said Margaret didn't look like that. Then she said her *mudder* told her not to come."

"I thought she wasn't telling anyone she was coming."

Ettie shrugged. "Must've changed her mind."

The music stopped, and a man with white and red trimmed robes stood at the front and said a few words. Ettie was too pre-occupied looking at the crowd to listen. More people came into the small church, and soon every seat was filled. When people lined the walls, Ettie glanced out the door to see even more people outside.

Ettie noticed Brandy sitting in the front row next to an older man. On the other side of the elderly man sat a young woman. Ettie figured that the old man had to be Norman Cartwright, the man Margaret was going to marry. Perhaps the younger woman was the daughter who jealously guarded her inheritance.

When the minister finished speaking, he stepped back,

and Norman Cartwright stood, introduced himself, and said a few words about the woman he had been set to marry. His words were heartfelt, and he appeared to be genuinely distressed. He had to stop twice while he wiped tears from his eyes.

When Norman finished, Brandy stood and said some nice things about Margo Rivers, who was formerly Margaret Yoder.

As soon as the service was over, Norman Cartwright stood up and headed over to them. He put out his hand and introduced himself. "Are you ladies relatives of Margo? She told me she was raised Amish."

"No we aren't, but her older sister is outside somewhere. She couldn't stay through the service." Ettie introduced everyone.

"Thank you for coming. I'm sure Margo would appreciate it. I might see if I can find her sister. What is her name?" Cartwright asked.

"Her name is Sarah," Ettie said.

Norman walked out of the church, and when Ettie glanced to the front, she could see Brandy looking around the crowd. Ettie lifted a hand and waved to her. Brandy smiled and waved back to the ladies.

Once everyone was outside, Ettie and Elsa-May walked amongst the crowd that had gathered. There were even two news crews. She spotted Detective Kelly with five people she recognized from his police station.

"There's Detective Kelly, and he's come with some officers. They're in plain clothes, but I can tell they're police."

"That was good of him to attend."

"Nice, but unusual of him to come with a group of his officers. Why would they take time out of their day to come to a funeral of someone they didn't know? I can understand one or two of them coming."

"The investigation is ongoing don't forget. They might be here to keep their eyes and ears open."

Ettie nodded. What Elsa-May said was most likely a reasonable explanation. But Detective Crowley would've attended funerals by himself so perhaps Kelly isn't as competent as their old detective was. Ettie took her attention off Kelly and looked around for Norman whom she saw talking with Sarah.

"We should listen in to what they're saying over there," Ettie said to Elsa-May nodding her head toward Norman and Sarah.

Ava overheard Ettie, and said, "I'll stand nearby to see if I can hear what they're saying."

Before Ettie could respond, Ava was walking toward Norman and Sarah.

"She's well trained," Elsa-May said with a smile. "Saves us doing it."

"Ettie, Elsa-May, it was good of you to be here."

Ettie smiled as she looked over at Brandy heading toward them. "Hello, Brandy."

"Hello. What you said about Margaret was very nice," Elsa-May commented.

"Do you think so? I was a little nervous. I've never spoken at a funeral before." She kept turning her head.

"Are you looking for someone?" Ettie asked.

"Just looking for Norman."

"He's over there talking with Sarah, Margaret's sister."

"I didn't think any of her family were coming," Brandy said.

"They told us they weren't coming. At least, her mother told us they wouldn't be coming."

Brandy peered over at Norman. "I wonder what they'd have to talk about."

"I imagine they're talking about Margaret. Sarah was too upset to stay through the service."

"Yes. He's a sympathetic person. It's always hard to know the right thing to say in these circumstances to make people feel better." Brandy looked in the opposite direction. "Oh, excuse me. I see someone I need to speak with."

When Brandy hurried away, Ettie looked back at Sarah and Norman. "It looks as though Ava is close enough to hear what they're saying. And it doesn't look like she's listening since she's sitting down in the only seat around."

"Are we going home now, or are we going to the graveyard? They announced it was a five minute drive," Elsa-May said.

"We might as well stay for the whole thing." Ettie looked up. "Norman and Sarah are walking toward us."

When Sarah reached them, she said, "Norman has been kind enough to offer us to go in one of his cars. He said he could fit us all in."

Mr. Cartwright said, "Ava and Sarah can come with me, and you can travel in the other car with my daughter, Paisley, and Brandy."

"Thank you. We'd appreciate that since we came by taxi," Elsa-May said.

A hush fell over the crowd, and everyone looked on as four men carried the coffin out the door of the church, and then placed it in the hearse.

"This way, ladies," Norman said once the coffin was in the hearse.

Ettie waved Ava over, and she hurried toward them.

"Norman has arranged for you and Sarah to go in the car with him and Ettie and I are going in another car with Brandy and Paisley," Elsa-May informed Ava.

The cars weren't ordinary cars they were long black limousines. Ettie had seen these kinds of cars at *Englisch* funerals before.

When they were driving to the grave, Brandy seemed put out. "Paisley and I traveled to the church in Norman's car. Now that all of you are here, Paisley and I are in this car."

"It's all the same to me," Paisley said as she lit up a cigarette.

"Do you mind, Paisley? I don't want to smell like an ashtray," Brandy sat across from Paisley, glaring at her.

Paisley rolled her eyes and stubbed the cigarette out in the ashtray that was built into the door beside her. "I don't know how I'll get through the day without another ciggy."

"You can light up when we get out of the car," Brandy snapped at her.

"I hope we haven't ruined things for you," Ettie said to Brandy. "You sound upset that you're not going in the car with Norman."

Brandy laughed, but Ettie knew it was a forced laugh and not a genuine one. "Don't be silly. What could you have ruined?"

"Yes, it's kind of him to show Sarah so much respect since she's the only member of Margaret's family here," Elsa-May said.

"Yes, he's good like that. He's such a gentleman." Brandy pulled out a mirrored compact and stared at her reflection. Then she pulled out lipstick and applied it. After that, she took a photo of herself with her mobile phone.

Ettie wondered whether Elsa-May would think Brandy's behavior a little strange.

Brandy shifted uncomfortably in the plush leather seat. "I just like being there for Norman in his time of need. He's such a good man."

"It's all the same to me," Paisley said. "It's just another day, another funeral. I'm only here to support my father."

"Do you go to many funerals?" Ettie asked.

"No, not really. I suppose I go to one every year or so. Mostly people my father knew and I have to go with him."

"You didn't know Margo very well, then?" Elsa-May asked.

"The point is that I *did* know her, probably even more so than my father did. I told him I thought he was making a mistake by marrying her, and I'll make no secret of that. I let everyone know what I thought of her and what she was after."

"How did you know her more than your father, since they were engaged to marry?" Ettie asked.

"I knew her type, and that's all I need to know. I've seen them come and go before." Paisley stared out the window.

"And what type is that?" Elsa-May asked.

Paisley shrugged as she looked over at Elsa-May. "It doesn't matter now. If I say too much, I'll be speaking ill of the dead. You ladies felt differently about her than I did, otherwise you wouldn't be at her funeral."

Elsa-May and Ettie nodded.

"We haven't seen her for years, so we don't really know her," Elsa-May explained.

Ettie leaned forward. "We're here more out of respect."

"Paisley and Margo didn't get along," Brandy explained.

Elsa-May smiled. "We guessed that."

"It wasn't too hard to tell," Ettie added.

Paisley turned her head away from the window to stare at Brandy. "You didn't like her either, Brandy, and don't pretend you did. Just be honest for once."

Brandy looked taken aback but giggled nervously, and then explained to the elderly sisters, "She was my intern, as you know. We had a business relationship; that didn't mean we had to be friends."

Paisley asked, "How did you ladies know Margo? You said you hadn't seen her in years, and you mentioned you're not relatives of hers."

"She came from our community, and she was found murdered outside Ettie's house when she was having an open house. Brandy was supposed to be doing the open house but made different plans at the last moment."

Paisley looked at Brandy. "How convenient."

"Sad is what it is. She had so much potential in her personal life and as an agent," Brandy said looking down.

"That's not what you told me. You said she was constantly distracted and didn't have her mind on the job." Paisley turned to the ladies. "Brandy complained that Margo had her mind on attracting my father and not on real estate. She wasn't good at the job at all."

"I do expect a lot from my interns. One hundred and ten percent is what I expect from them."

Elsa-May leaned toward Brandy. "You can only get one hundred percent because that would be their maximum."

"I do know that, Elsa-May."

"Then why say it if you know it's not right? I've often heard people say people are giving something one hundred and ten percent, or one hundred and twenty percent, and I have to tell you that I do find it irritating."

"I'm sorry to irritate you, Elsa-May. I'll never say one hundred and ten percent again," Brandy stated flatly.

"Thank you. It's only proper that you don't."

Brandy arched an eyebrow. "I see that I'll have to watch what I say around you two."

"Not me, only Elsa-May," Ettie said.

CHAPTER 9

WHEN THE CARS pulled up at the graveyard, Ettie was certain that Brandy was going to hurry over to catch up with Norman, but she didn't. Brandy stayed with Ettie and Elsa-May as they slowly walked to the open grave while Paisley joined her father.

Everyone stood in silence until the crowd of people had re-assembled by the coffin, which was now by the open grave. The minister said a few words from the Bible, and another man said a prayer before the coffin was lowered. Norman stepped forward and threw a single pink rose onto the top of the coffin.

Ettie wiped away a single tear. It was sad to see such a young life wasted and causing so much sadness for those who loved her.

Even Brandy was patting under her eyes with a tissue. Ettie looked at Norman's daughter who'd remained stony-faced; most of her face was hidden under large-rimmed dark sunglasses. It was clear she'd had no respect for Margaret, and couldn't find any sympathy for her father's loss.

Sarah was on the opposite side of the grave from Ettie and Elsa-May. Once Sarah began to sob, Ava put her arm around her and walked with her away from the grave.

"Must be hard for Sarah." Just as Ettie had whispered that to Elsa-May, a familiar figure caught her eye. It was Josh Tomson. "Look, Elsa-May, over there; it's Josh."

Elsa-May glanced over her shoulder and then turned back around. "He must've come to pay his respects in private. Most likely waiting until we all go."

"Don't let on we know he's there."

"That's probably best," Elsa-May agreed.

"I've been trying to catch the detective's eye to say hello, but he's deliberately staying away. He's purposely not looking at us."

"Well, ignore him. He obviously doesn't want people to know that we know him too well."

"You must be right."

"I mostly am," Elsa-May added. "I thought I was wrong once, but I was mistaken."

"Sh," Ettie said.

They turned back toward the grave to see Norman fall to his knees sobbing. His daughter kneeled down with him and did her best to comfort him.

"The poor man," Ettie said, "he's devastated."

When the minister walked over to him, Norman pushed himself to his feet. The minister said a few words to him while he touched him on the shoulder lightly. When it was over, the sisters looked on from a distance, and the crowd dispersed.

"We should have someone call us a taxi; I don't want to stay on for a meal or drinks, or whatever," Ettie said to Elsa-May, who agreed.

ETTIE AND ELSA-MAY were pleased to be home by themselves. They'd taken Sarah and Ava home on the way.

While they boiled the pot on the stove for a much-needed cup of hot tea, Elsa-May sat stroking Snowy, who was being unusually quiet.

"It's a shame Ava didn't find out anything useful. Norman and Sarah weren't talking about anything other than what Margaret was like as a girl."

"I must say I'd find it very hard to think that Norman was guilty or involved in some way. What about you?"

"I agree. I don't think anyone can fake the way he broke down at her funeral. Unless he was feeling guilty; guilt could look like grief."

"What about the daughter, Paisley? She was very straight-faced throughout the whole thing, and she made it known she didn't like Margaret one bit."

"She's pleased her father's not going to marry someone she probably regarded as a 'gold digger,' but that doesn't mean she killed her or had her killed."

"Maybe not, but it was convenient for her. Brandy said Paisley wasn't happy about the upcoming marriage, and now it isn't going to happen."

"Did you notice how Brandy was with Norman? She was upset about not traveling in the car with him. I wouldn't be surprised if she was sweet on him."

SAMANTHA PRICE

"I think he's just a client she wants to keep happy. You know what she's like. It's a wonder she's even bothering with a house the value of yours, but then again, she wasn't. She had her intern hold the open house."

Ettie's face fell. "I suppose you're right. I think she only took my house on as a favor to Ruth. She's been a customer of Ruth's bakery for years."

"That'll be the pot boiling, Ettie. You make the tea while Snowy's being so quiet."

Ettie laughed. "Okay, you sit there and have a rest."

When Ettie came back with a cup of tea, Elsa-May put Snowy down so she could take the tea from Ettie. "Didn't we have to tell Detective Kelly what Josh said to you?"

"Jah, I should have gone there before now. I'm surprised he hasn't called in to see us. I know he'll have us talk to him again, now that Ava told us that Josh and Margaret met regularly."

"We should go tomorrow. I half thought he might have spoken to us at the funeral, but it was good of him to leave that note on the door telling us where and when the funeral would be."

"It was good of him to go out of his way to let us know. That's true."

Elsa-May slurped on her tea.

Ettie had given up asking her to stop drinking like that. She knew Elsa-May would only tell her it tasted better like that.

CHAPTER 10

ETTIE AND ELSA-MAY waited at the police station to see Detective Kelly.

"Do you know exactly what you're going to say to him, Ettie?"

"*Jah*, what Josh said to us. And Josh was at the funeral when no other Amish people besides us four women were. None of Margaret's family, besides Sarah, was there. Do you think Kelly noticed Josh there? There were so many people he might not have seen him."

"This way, ladies."

They both looked up to see Detective Kelly motioning with his finger for them to follow him.

As soon as they sat down in his office, he began by asking, "What did you manage to find out for me, Ettie?"

"We happened to see Josh at the Sunday meeting, and we talked with him. I didn't feel comfortable stopping by to see him at his home because we don't know him that well."

Elsa-May nodded. "That's right; we've got nothing in

common with the young man, like Ettie said, so why would we visit him?"

The detective ignored Elsa-May. "So what did you find out, Ettie?"

"He said he hasn't seen Margaret since she left the community."

"He also said people have told him things about her, and they said the man she was going to marry was a dishonest person."

"Dishonest? In what way? There are lots of ways to be dishonest, some ways worse than others," the detective commented.

"He didn't actually say, and I don't recall that we asked him," Elsa-May said.

"He's a businessman and in business there is often a winner and a loser, and often the losers are sore. Many people have rumors about them being dishonest."

Elsa-May leaned forward and jutted out her bottom jaw. "So have you heard anything about Norman Cartwright being unscrupulous?"

"I wouldn't use that word. But many people go as far as they can; they stretch the law without breaking it, if you know what I mean."

"Go as far as they can and still stay within the law?" Elsa-May asked.

"Correct. Well, as far as we know, that is."

Elsa-May stared at Ettie. "Tell him what else we know."

"He was at her funeral."

"Who?"

"Josh Tomson. He wasn't at the service portion of the

funeral; he came to the grave. He could've been at the service come to think of it. There were so many people they couldn't all fit in the church."

"I know, I was there," the detective stated.

"Josh stayed back a distance so no one would see him," Elsa-May said.

"He most likely didn't want to speak to anyone, Elsa-May. You make it sound like he's guilty of something. Anyway, we saw him. I think he was waiting until everyone left so he could be with her in peace."

"Yes, I saw him there too," Kelly repeated.

"He never got over her leaving him," Ettie said.

"Is that so? And how do you know this?" Kelly asked.

"Everyone knew," Elsa-May added.

"Mrs. Smith, I want you to go back and talk to Josh for me one more time."

Ettie's face contorted. That was the last thing she wanted to do. Josh was so upset that she didn't want to keep speaking with him about Margaret.

"I think that's something that Ettie would rather not do, Detective."

"Elsa-May's right," Ettie said. "You see, he's feeling a huge loss right now. I hardly know him, too, which makes things more difficult."

"It would help me; more importantly, it will help him. Otherwise, suspicion will be thrown onto him as I told you before. Nothing you've said so far puts him in the clear in my mind," the detective said.

"Why would you be suspicious of him at all?"

"I can't tell you that at this point, Ettie."

"You told Ettie you would speak with him once she

talked to him and now she has. Why do you want her to do it all over again? It doesn't make sense."

Ettie was pleased Elsa-May was saying things to the detective that she wasn't brave enough to say to him herself.

"I know I said all those things. I'm certain he lied about not seeing her recently." He sighed. "I suppose I can tell you this much; we've obtained Margaret's phone records and according to them, she *has* spoken to him. We've found that she's been calling a number which is in Josh Tomson's name between two and three times a week in recent times."

Ettie and Elsa-May exchanged a shocked glance. Josh had lied to them.

"Well that's something we didn't know," Elsa-May said.

"Quite disturbing really," Ettie agreed.

"Do you see my dilemma, ladies?"

Elsa-May nodded. "We did hear some gossip that they met regularly in town."

The detective's jaw dropped open. "Why didn't you tell me? This is the kind of thing I need to know."

"We were going to tell you. We weren't keeping it from you."

He shook his head and scowled at them. "It sounds like you were keeping it from me to throw suspicion off him. Now that you know he lied you might be more inclined to be more open with me. I need you to ask him a few more questions."

Elsa-May groaned. "You're looking in the wrong direction if you think Josh had anything to do with this."

The detective put both hands to his head. "Is this the

old thing that you ladies think an Amish person can't be guilty? Because they can. People are people; it doesn't matter what they believe."

Ettie studied the detective's face and wondered what to say to him. How could she explain things that had to be understood with the heart? The detective was being too scientific and mathematical about things. "But don't you believe there is a certain type of person that is a murderer?"

"No, Mrs. Smith. I don't. Certainly there are people more prone to killing people willy-nilly, but when people are pushed the wrong way or too hard, you'll be surprised what they're capable of."

"Going along that line of reasoning, Detective, what scenario would you come up with for someone being pushed to kill Margaret?"

Ettie stared at Elsa-May wondering what she was talking about. She didn't want to sit there and listen to reasons why people might want to kill others. Now she'd be stuck there for the next ten minutes or so listening while the detective waffled on. She'd certainly have a word with her sister as soon as they got out of his office.

"I'd say this was a crime of jealousy because Josh was rejected several times by a beautiful woman and she was about to marry the richest man in a five-hundred-mile radius of here. That would be hard for any man to take particularly when she'd been all set to marry him years ago."

"Wouldn't he have put that all behind him, though? From all their phone calls it would appear that they'd become friends rather than enemies."

"That's exactly why I want you to speak with him again, Mrs. Smith." He clapped his hands in the air so loud that Ettie and Elsa-May jumped.

Ettie was trapped; she had no way out but to go through with the detective's request.

"I will talk to him," Ettie said. "But I can't say that I will speak with him anytime soon. He'll know something is up if we visit him because that's something that we normally would not do. A couple of ladies of our age would not visit a couple of young men. Now if he was still living with his family that would be a different story. We could stop by the family's house with no qualms, couldn't we, Elsa-May?"

"Yes we go visiting all the time, but we've got nothing in common with Josh so it would just be odd."

"I see. So you'd feel you have to wait for a suitable function?" the detective asked.

"Yes or even our next meeting every second Sunday. The next one's not too far away, and you still haven't got your toxicology report back yet, have you?" Ettie asked.

"That's still at least a week away," the detective said.

"Where are you up to with your other investigations? Do you have any other leads?"

"I just want you ladies to concentrate on Josh and the information he might have."

"Since this happened at my house I would feel more comfortable if you let us know what you find out, Detective."

"Yes, don't you owe Ettie that since she's helping you with your investigations?"

The detective held both hands up. "All right, all right.

I'm not only investigating Josh; I'm looking into everyone involved. Everyone in Margaret's life."

Elsa-May leaned forward. "Who?"

The detective answered, "Norman's daughter, Paisley, and Brandy."

Ettie gasped. "Brandy?"

"Surely you don't think she had anything to do with this?" Elsa-May asked.

"No, of course not, but everyone has to be investigated so they can be eliminated."

"Brandy told us the daughter wasn't happy about her father marrying Margaret. You told us that you had her coming in for questioning?" Ettie asked.

"I did some days ago, and we got her DNA for elimination purposes. Margaret was only one year older than she was. I suppose that would be hard for any child to take. Norman's ex-wife lives in California. Norman and his ex-wife, Candice, haven't spoken to each other in years."

"Is Paisley close to her mother?" Ettie asked.

"Paisley didn't have much to do with her father growing up. Her mother raised her in California. According to Paisley, her mother didn't mind her moving here when she was eighteen to commence working for her father."

"Well, it seems she wasn't just any child going to live with her father since her father was so wealthy," Elsa-May said.

The detective nodded. "That's another factor in this whole thing."

"One thing you haven't mentioned again, Detective, is the missing ring."

He stared at Ettie. "Where did you find out about the ring?"

"You told us about the ring before."

Elsa-May added, "We saw her finger, it was red and swollen. And we knew that was the finger where wedding rings are generally placed. Then when we found out she was engaged to a wealthy man, we just put two and two together. Like Ettie said, you told us all about it the other day."

The detective rubbed his jaw. "Yes, I remember now. Her ring was missing; that's quite right. We've notified all the usual places someone might try to offload a diamond of that size, but so far we've drawn a blank."

"A ring like that would most likely stand out. It's not an everyday kind of ring by the sounds of it," Elsa-May said.

"Quite right. The other possibility would be that the diamond could be recut, and the laser identification would be lost. It would lose some of its carat weight, but that would be made up for because it could be sold untraceable on the open market. It wouldn't have to be sold under the table."

"Sounds like you've got your work cut out for you," Ettie said.

"It's been a tough one so far. That's why I appreciate any help you can give me."

Elsa-May stared at the detective. "Did they make it known how much the ring was worth? Did Margaret tell anyone her ring was of so much value?"

"I've asked that question of Norman already. That was one of the first things I asked him."

AMISH MURDER TOO CLOSE

"And what was his answer?" Elsa-May asked.

"They were careful not to tell people what the diamond in her ring was worth through fear of something like this happening."

"Did Margaret have any close friends?

"Not that we've been able to find out about. Brandy knew of no one close to her."

"Where did he get a diamond of that size? I'm guessing it's not a thing you'd purchase from a local jeweler."

"It was sourced by a New York gem dealer. I've already been to see him, and he's verified everything that Norman told me about the diamond. I've got copies of all the paperwork and laboratory certificates."

"So you're still not certain whether Margaret was killed for the diamond or for some other reason?" Ettie asked tilting her head.

"If we can't find a personal reason, it would most likely be for the stone since it was worth so much."

"We should go now." Ettie stood. "We'll be back in touch once we speak to Josh again."

The detective stood. "I do appreciate your help in all this."

Ettie and Elsa-May hurried out of his office.

"What's the big hurry, Ettie?"

"I think we should go to see Josh because he lied to us about Margaret."

"Go to his *haus?*"

"Why not?"

"That was the last thing you wanted to do the other day. You told Kelly we were going to wait until we saw him again," Elsa-May said.

"I've rethought things. Now we've got a reason to see Josh."

Elsa-May shook her head, and deep lines appeared on her forehead. "But we don't want him to know the detective's sent us. If we show up on his doorstep upset with him for keeping information from us, that'll look odd."

"Do you have a better idea, Elsa-May?"

"We already said that we'll wait until we see him again."

"What if we take him a pie?"

Elsa-May laughed. "A pie?"

"Two single men living on their own would appreciate a pie, and we can take it there later tonight when they're certain to be home."

"If that's what you want to do, Ettie, I'll come with you as always."

"Let's go. We've got baking to do."

CHAPTER 11

"THE SECRET to a good apple pie is the filling, and also the pastry," Ettie stated.

"So the secret is the filling and the crust? Then, there's nothing left; that's hardly a baking secret. In fact, what you just said makes no sense at all." Elsa-May continued peeling the apples for the pie with Ettie beside her.

Ettie did her best to explain further. "The way I see it, the filling has to be tasty and firm – not runny, and the pastry can't be too doughy or too dry." Ettie broke off a slice of apple and popped it into her mouth. "Oooh. Have you tasted these?"

"*Nee,* why?"

"They're not sweet they're sour."

"I like using sour apples."

"Well, I don't!"

"That could be a big problem." Elsa-May popped a small piece of apple into her mouth. "That's quite tart. We could add a lot of sugar if you want the pie that sweet."

"Do you think that'll help? We'll have to add a lot."

"We'll taste it before we put it into the pastry to make sure it tastes all right."

They hadn't been to the store for days, so they were left with the apples from Bernie next door who had given them some from the two trees in his yard.

The apples were stewed in sweet liquid until they were firm. When they were both happy with the taste, the filling was added to the pastry crust that lined the pie tin. Once the filling was heaped high, Ettie placed the rolled out top layer onto the pie. To finish it off, Ettie decorated the center with small pieces of pastry fashioned into a flower.

After the pie was placed in the oven, both sisters walked into their living room to have a much-needed rest.

Ettie closed her eyes. *Why would someone want Margaret dead?* Several scenarios ran through her mind.

The next thing Ettie was aware of was being shaken awake by Elsa-May.

"Ettie, wake up we have a visitor."

Ettie opened her eyes to see Detective Crowley sitting in front of her. She coughed and sat straight on the couch. "Detective, is it you or am I dreaming?"

"He's here because he read the papers, Ettie."

"So nice of you to visit us. Have you talked to Detective Kelly?"

He shook his head. "No, I haven't. I wanted to see how you two are holding up. I recognized your house from the photo in the paper, Ettie."

"Yes, it was a dreadful thing. I don't know what they said in the papers; did you know that the girl used to be Amish and was raised in our community?"

"The paper didn't mention anything of the kind. I'm sorry to hear that; that makes it doubly awful for you. Was she someone you knew well?"

"We knew her, but she left us five years ago. She'd been working with the real estate company for a year."

"So she was there to sell your house that your friend left you, Ettie?"

"Yes. I had intended to sell it. I don't know what will happen with it now that there's been another murder there."

Elsa-May said, "The realtor Ettie had selling her place had her intern do the open house, and the intern was the one killed. Her name was Margaret Yoder."

"And Brandy Winnie, the woman she was an intern for, had Margaret change her name to Margo Rivers thinking it sounded like a better name for a realtor."

"That is interesting. I guess that's not a good thing for the sale of the house," Crowley said.

"There's nothing anyone can do about that now."

"Would you like tea, Detective?"

"Yes, I would thank you, Elsa-May."

"While you're in there, it smells like that pie's ready to come out of the oven."

Elsa-May laughed. "It's been out of the oven for about half an hour now. I got it out while you were sleeping."

"Just as well you were awake, then."

Elsa-May stood up. "I'll make the tea and see what I can find for us to eat."

"Sounds good," Crowley said.

"I don't know what you read in the paper, but the girl

didn't have any of her money or cards stolen; the only thing that was taken was her engagement ring."

"How much do you know about her?" Crowley asked.

"Just that she was the youngest child of Gideon and Rose Yoder, she was not far from marrying a man years ago, and then she called off the wedding and left the community."

The former detective rubbed his chin. "Is that all you know about her?"

"Why? Is there something else we should know?"

"No, I don't believe so. The most obvious things is—did she have any enemies?"

"Well, that's the confusing thing. Were they after Margaret or Brandy? Brandy was the one who should've been there that day running the open house. It was her name in the newspaper advertisement. Margaret was Brandy's intern, and Brandy had Margaret do the open house at short notice. They both looked similar although Brandy's older."

"Let's start with Margaret; did *she* have any enemies?"

"She was about to be married to a very wealthy man."

Crowley nodded. "Yes, I read in the paper she was engaged to Norman Cartwright. He's worth millions."

"That's correct and according to Brandy his daughter wasn't happy about splitting her inheritance down the middle. The daughter thought Margaret, or Margo as they knew her, was a gold digger."

"And did Brandy have any enemies?" he asked.

"She's not certain, but she did say that she has people who aren't happy with her from time to time over real-estate deals—people who miss out on properties."

"I tend to think that it would be unlikely that they were after Brandy."

Elsa-May came back with the tea and a tray of cookies. "Did I hear you say that you don't think the killer was after Brandy?"

"Yes." Crowley nodded.

"Why's that?" Elsa-May set the tea on the table and sat back down.

"When it comes to murder, cases of mistaken identity are rare. Unless Margaret was driving Brandy's car. Was she?"

"No, she wasn't." Ettie shook her head.

"It might have been an option if she were driving someone else's car. Yes, I doubt very much they were after Brandy."

"That's good to know."

"Thank you, Detective. We didn't quite see things that way. What you're saying makes sense."

Ettie looked over at Elsa-May. "Well, am I going to pour the tea?"

Elsa-May pushed herself up off the chair. "I was just giving it a little time to steep. You would've complained if I poured it straightaway, but I didn't. I just can't win with you, Ettie."

Ettie giggled.

"I can see not too much has changed," Crowley said in an amused tone.

"Not too much ever changes around here," Elsa-May said.

"And how are things going with you?" Ettie asked Crowley.

"I've taken up golf. It's challenging, and it gives me something to do."

Elsa-May passed Crowley a cup of tea and then handed one to Ettie before she sat back down.

"That's good that you've found something you like to do," Ettie said.

The detective brought the cup to his lips and took a sip. "I had thought about getting back into detective work on a part-time basis."

"That would be a good idea," Ettie said.

"I'd take private clients, which would most likely be missing persons cases and things like that."

"That sounds like it would suit you and with your connections in the police force, many people would like to hire you."

"Do you think so?"

"Of course," Ettie said. "You can practice right now."

"I'd be happy to."

Ettie and Elsa-May told Crowley everything they knew about the facts surrounding the murder of the woman who died with the name Margo Rivers.

"It does seem very odd that she would wear the ring seeing it was worth so much money. She'd almost need to go around with a bodyguard beside her. Often when people own a valuable ring like that they wear a replica and keep the real one in the safe."

"Detective Kelly said something like that, and that's an interesting point. Was she wearing a fake?"

"Or what if she was wearing the replica and that was stolen? Someone could have thought it was the real thing," Ettie said.

Crowley frowned. "Cartwright should've been able to clear that up right away, whether she was wearing a fake."

Elsa-May shook her head. "He mentioned nothing about it. From what the detective said, the man Margaret was going to marry had the ring insured."

"He could be taking advantage of the robbery to claim insurance on a fake ring," Ettie said.

"Do you think he'd be in the right mind to think that fast right after his fiancée died?" Crowley suggested.

"You really think he would take advantage of the situation to collect an insurance payout, Ettie?" Elsa-May asked.

"Do you?" Ettie deflected the question to Crowley, who remained silent while staring at her. "What are you thinking?" Ettie eventually asked him.

"I'm just mulling the whole thing over. I've heard the ring was worth nearly a million dollars so that would be a sizeable payout. There are various scenarios. Number one; someone could have taken the ring thinking it was the real deal. Number two; Cartwright could be taking advantage of the situation of her dying and the ring missing. Only he'd know if the missing ring was fake or real. And that doesn't have to mean he had anything to do with her death."

"And are there any more scenarios?" Elsa-May asked.

The former detective shook his head. "That's actually the only two I can think of that make sense. If Norman was growing tired of Margaret, he could've broken the engagement and legally he would've been entitled to get the ring back since the marriage hadn't taken place."

"You're saying if he wanted the ring back he wouldn't

have to kill her? Neither would he need to have someone kill her to take the ring whether she was wearing the fake one or not."

"Correct," Crowley said. "If he's involved in this illegally, the scenario would be she was wearing a fake ring, and he's going to make a claim."

"I'd think he would be too upset to do anything like that. You should've seen him at the funeral," Elsa-May said.

Crowley chuckled. "Don't be fooled by things like that. I've seen many good actors in my time. When I started out in my young days, I used to believe what people told me. If someone looked me in the eye and said something, I believed them. That didn't last long. Now I let the evidence speak, and I'm not swayed by how people act."

Ettie tilted her head to one side. "And what about the daughter? Could she have killed Margaret and stolen the ring to make it look like a robbery and a homicide?"

"That's possible, but I say all this without knowing what evidence Kelly's sitting on. From what you've said, Margaret sounds like she was a woman with few friends. Maybe that's why she carried on a friendship with her former fiancé from your community. Does the daughter have a mother somewhere? Does Cartwright have an ex-wife? She might not be too happy about her daughter losing out on an inheritance."

"We've not given much thought to Paisley's mother. She lives in California or somewhere far away."

"What do you make of Josh lying to us saying he had no contact with her? Kelly told us that they had regular phone conversations, and then Ava said her husband told her that Josh had even met with Margaret."

"No one likes to be jilted, Ettie, and it most likely made him feel a fool. Why would he admit his shortcomings?" Crowley stared at the two sisters.

"Elsa-May and I are going to take Josh a pie and mention that we heard he met Margaret in town."

"We have to be careful not to mention that the detective knows about the phone calls because we're not supposed to know about that," Elsa-May said.

"We're going to find out why he didn't mention that he met her in town."

"When did Detective Kelly say he would speak to him?" Crowley asked.

"After we find out a few things from him. He's never had any success talking to people in the community. They just clam up on him."

"He shouldn't let that stand in his way of finding things out. It's a shame Margaret didn't have any close friends," Crowley said.

"Yes, it is."

Elsa-May leaned forward. "From what we've told you, who do you think might have killed her?"

He shrugged. "Going on the information at hand, all likelihood points to the daughter. That is, if I have to guess." He laughed. "But it sounds like there's not enough information just yet. And I say the daughter, simply because I don't know all the facts."

"I wonder how we could find more out about the ring. Would the same person who sold him the diamond have made the replica? Assuming there was one?" Elsa-May asked repositioning herself in her chair.

"According to the newspaper, the stone was sourced from a diamond broker in New York. A jeweler the broker recommended, most likely made the ring that held the diamond. That jeweler could quite possibly have made a replica to go along with the real ring."

"Kelly said he visited the broker already, and the broker confirmed everything Norman told Kelly," Ettie said wondering if she'd already told him that.

"Are you going to visit Kelly?"

"Yes, I will. This case has me intrigued."

CHAPTER 12

WHEN THE FORMER DETECTIVE LEFT, Ettie closed her eyes again.

"Ettie, we should go now if you still want to visit Josh."

Ettie opened her eyes, and then blinked hard. "I'm tired now after Crowley's visit. Do you still think we should go, or leave it for tomorrow?"

"Jah, come on. Let's do it and see what we can find out."

"I'm a little less enthusiastic about going to see him now that I've found out that Crowley thinks it's the daughter who killed her."

"He didn't say that. He only meant based on all the information at hand. I'm sure there's so much more we don't know."

Ettie laughed. "There usually is."

"I can go by myself if you want to stay home and have a nap."

"Nee, I'm coming." Ettie grabbed a cookie off the plate before she took hold of her shawl by the door. "Let's go."

When Elsa-May didn't join her, Ettie looked around to see Elsa-May with her arms folded. "What's wrong now?"

"Are you forgetting the pie?"

Ettie had forgotten all about the pie, but she wasn't going to let Elsa-May know that. "I thought you would bring it. Haven't you got it packed up ready to go yet?"

Elsa-May rolled her eyes as she walked into the kitchen. "Just a moment," she called out.

When Elsa-May had the pie packed up, they walked to the shanty down the road and called for a taxi. It was a ten-minute drive in the taxi to where Josh lived with Arthur Gosling.

WHEN THE TAXI stopped right outside the house, they saw both men in a wagon as though they had just pulled up at their house. Arthur and Josh jumped down from the wagon and headed toward the taxi.

"We've made you some pie," Elsa-May said clutching the pie in front of her.

"*Denke,* Elsa-May," Arthur said taking the pie from her. "We can always do with pie. He glanced over at Ettie, who was still getting out of the taxi. "Do you need a hand, Ettie?"

"I'm quite all right."

Arthur waited until Ettie had nearly reached him before he said, "Come inside. Would you like to stay for the evening meal?"

"*Nee denke.* We couldn't, could we?" Elsa-May looked at Ettie.

"Actually, we need to get back and walk the dog and work in the garden. It's been so hot lately, and we like to do it in the cool of the evening."

"I'll put the pot on to boil." Arthur glanced over at Josh. "Are you coming inside?"

"I'll be there soon; just fixing a few things up here."

Both ladies waved hello to Josh.

Arthur continued to the house. "We don't get many visitors around here, so this is a special occasion."

Unfortunately for the two sisters, the wrong man was the one doing the talking. They'd come to see Josh, not Arthur, but Josh was still outside tending to the horse and the wagon.

"Kaffe?" Arthur asked as he walked into the kitchen with them following.

"Jah, please," the two sisters said at the same time.

"We have lots of cookies," he said tipping some into a plate from a bowl.

Just as Arthur was placing the coffee in front of them, Josh walked in the door. He took his hat off and then sat down with them.

Ettie wished she'd planned some way of bringing up Margaret's name. It was made doubly hard with Arthur Gosling in the room. It didn't look like Arthur was going anywhere as he'd placed a mug on the table for each of them including himself.

Just as Ettie thought she'd have to abandon their mission, Arthur unknowingly did her a favor. "I heard the dreadful news about Margaret Yoder being found near Agatha's old house. You two were the ones who found her?"

"Yes, it was awful. Mind you, we didn't recognize her at all. She'd changed so much," Ettie said.

Elsa-May leaned over and said to Josh, "You would've recognized her because you met regularly with her, didn't you?"

Ettie was rather shocked by Elsa-May's straightforward approach especially since Josh had already told them that he'd not seen her since she left the community—and left him—weeks before their wedding.

Josh looked a little startled; so he couldn't back out, Ettie added, "That's what we were told by someone."

He looked down into his coffee and back up to Ettie. *"Jah,* I did meet with her sometimes. She called and needed my help."

"What with?" Elsa-May asked, now looking more relaxed while she sipped on her coffee.

"Anything and everything. She felt she didn't belong where she was, and she didn't belong here in the community either. She needed someone to discuss things with. I didn't want to get involved with anything to do with the police or her murder. She's gone now, and that's that. I don't know anything."

Ettie had believed him up until he added that last bit about him not knowing anything. He had offered information that they hadn't asked about. In Ettie's view, that had always translated as meaning a person *did* know something. *But what could he know?*

"Naturally, we were confused when you said that you hadn't seen her and then we found you met with her regularly," Elsa-May said, tactfully not mentioning the fact that he'd lied.

"Seems you're taking quite an interest, Elsa-May," Arthur said bringing his coffee mug to his mouth.

"We were the ones who found her body and it was right outside Ettie's *haus*." Elsa-May shook her head. "No one should go that way. Why wouldn't we take an interest?"

"It was a shock for us," Ettie added. "As I'm sure it would've been for you too, Josh, to find out she'd been taken so quickly."

He nodded and stared into his coffee. "It was. I was praying she wouldn't marry that man and that she'd come back. When she first contacted me, months ago, I thought she would say she was coming back, but it wasn't to be."

"Half your prayers were answered," Arthur said with a laugh.

Josh scowled at him. "That's not funny, Arthur."

"Nee, it's not. I'm sorry. I'll leave you three to talk. I didn't know Margaret really well, so I'll take my *kaffe* and go check on the livestock."

They waited until he'd left the room to talk some more.

"I hope we haven't made Arthur feel awkward," Elsa-May said. "Perhaps I said something to upset him?"

Josh shook his head. *"Nee* he just never knows the right thing to say at the right time; he means no harm."

"Getting back to Margaret, how did she contact you the first time after she left?" Ettie asked.

"She called me on the phone. I was still living with my parents at the time. They'd had several calls where they'd answered, and the person had hung up. I thought it might be Margaret, so I stayed by the barn in case she called again. When I answered, she spoke. We met once or twice and then we met more frequently."

"Only in this past year?"

"Jah. How did you know?"

"Just a guess," Ettie said.

"I know it wasn't the wisest thing for me to do to talk to her like that, but I was in love and couldn't say no to her." He put his head in his hands and sobbed.

Ettie looked at Elsa-May, wondering what they should do or say.

Elsa-May patted him on the shoulder. "There, there, it's alright."

"I don't see how it can be; she's gone. There will never be anybody like her again. Not for me. I'd been praying that she'd come back, and I thought for a while that *Gott* had finally heard my prayers." Through tear-filled eyes he looked at Elsa-May. "But He didn't answer my prayers. He took her away from me for good."

"It's hard to know why our prayers aren't always answered," Elsa-May said.

"I don't mind telling you that this has rocked my faith."

"Have you spoken to the bishop about it?"

"He wouldn't be able to understand. He's never lost anyone he's loved; he wouldn't understand what I'm going through. I feel I've lost her three times not just once. I lost her the first time when she left me. The second time was when I thought she might come back to me, and she didn't, and then the third and final time was when she died. She's gone forever."

"We just have to trust that God knows what's best for

us. His ways are higher than our ways, and His thoughts are not our thoughts, and neither can we know them."

Ettie sat there not knowing what to say to comfort Josh. She'd often wondered herself why God seems to favor one person over another. Josh had his share of grief and what for? She considered Elsa-May was doing a far better job of comforting him than she could've done.

He shook his head. "It's hard to keep believing when your prayers are never answered."

"It only seems like they aren't being answered, but they are; I'm certain of it. You'll look back on this in a year or two, and you'll see that you went through all these hard times for a reason. You've got things to learn from this. Maybe *Gott* is teaching you to have great faith and have great patience. You'll be able to help others who go through this now since it has to be experienced to learn of it."

"I wish He'd find another way to do that. I've been in pain over Margaret for so long, believing she would come back to me, and she never did. If I hadn't believed in *Gott* so much, I wouldn't be having so much pain now. Do you see what I mean?"

As Josh sobbed into his fists, Elsa-May gave Ettie a desperate glance. Seemed like she'd run out of things to say to comfort him.

"Do you have anyone that you feel comfortable speaking with about this?" Ettie asked. "What about Jeremiah?"

"*Jah.* Jeremiah is a *gut* friend; I said a few things to him already. I guess I could talk to him."

"Jeremiah was lonely too, and he had no one in his life until Ava came along."

He sniffed and nodded. "I know. Everyone thought he'd never marry."

"And that's what they thought about Ava too," Ettie added.

Ettie nodded. "The way things are, Josh, we don't have any other choice but to trust Him. He's the one who knows the beginning from the end and answers our prayers and even the ones we've never asked. He knows what's good for us."

"I guess there's some reason that all this is happening to me. There has to be a reason."

"*Jah* there is. As I said, you'll look back on these hard times you're having and you'll know why you had to endure it. It's just very hard to go through it at that time. We've both lost our husbands and that's not easy. It's awful to have the person you're closest to in the world be snatched from you."

He looked across at the two sisters. "I know; that must be hard for both of you and everyone who has lost a spouse, but the difference is that you had that time with them. You had them for years, you got to have *kinner* with them, and that'll never be like that for me and Margaret."

"The plain truth of it is, Josh, you need to be with someone who wants to be with you. Margaret made her choice, and she left you, can't you see that? Don't you want to be with someone who doesn't want to be without you?" Elsa-May asked.

Ettie held her breath hoping Elsa-May's plain talking wouldn't bring on another onslaught of tears.

He put his hands down. "I do. I want to be with someone who's happy here in the community and wants to be with me. Margaret never felt at home here."

"That's right, so can you see a little clearer now? She was never the girl for you; not really." Elsa-May smiled at him and patted his arm.

He ran a hand through his wavy hair. "I suppose you're right. I always had it stuck in my head that she was the only one for me, but the perfect woman for me wouldn't have left me all those years ago."

Ettie relaxed with relief. Who would've thought Elsa-May's tongue could've made someone feel better?

Elsa-May smiled. "That's the way. That's the right way to look at things."

He chuckled and leaned back. "Look at me. I'm an idiot for crying. I haven't cried since I was five-years-old."

"Everyone needs a good cry every now and again," Elsa-May said.

"*Denke,* I do feel better. I'll make an effort to remember your words when I'm feeling down."

"We've all been down in the dumps. And we just have to pull ourselves out again. We're never alone," Ettie added.

He nodded and wiped his eyes with the back of his hand. "*Denke* for coming. You've made me feel better about things. There are so few people I can confide in. I've never been able to speak to my parents."

"You know where we live, so come and talk to us any time you like," Ettie said.

"*Denke,* I just might."

"*Gut.* What have you got for the evening meal? Ettie

SAMANTHA PRICE

and I just might do some cooking for you while we're here."

His face brightened. "That would be a treat. Will you both stay? I can drive you home after."

"Jah, denke, we'll stay."

CHAPTER 13

WHEN ETTIE and Elsa-May got home, they both fell exhausted onto Ettie's small couch while Snowy tried his best to jump up with them.

"If I wasn't tired before I am now. Did you have to offer to cook for Arthur and Josh?" Ettie asked.

"I did. And we've had our dinner, too, so no more cooking tonight I just felt sorry for them."

"Me too. I must say I thought what you said to Josh was very good, Elsa-May."

"Denke." Elsa-May chuckled.

"I could tell it comforted him greatly, especially when you helped him see that Margaret didn't love him enough to be happy with his commitment to life in the Amish community. It must be hard when people don't have anyone really close to talk with. We've got each other we can confide in."

"Everyone needs someone. That's how *Gott* made us. Every man needs a helpmeet."

"I suppose that's true. I do hope Josh finds himself a

nice girl. It'll make him feel so much better. I find it hard to believe he waited so long for Margaret to come back."

"Can't have helped that she kept talking to him and calling him," Elsa-May said.

"*Jah,*" Ettie agreed. "A clean break would've been better for him. What do you think she was talking to him about? We never really found that out." Ettie pulled a face. "We can't talk with him again."

"*Nee,* we can't. We can't bring up Margaret's name again."

"You rest on the couch, Elsa-May. I'll bring you a cup of hot tea."

"*Denke,* Ettie."

When Ettie came back with the tea, Elsa-May said, "I never realized how comfortable this couch is."

"It's mine. Don't get too comfortable." Ettie laughed. "No one likes coming here to sit in those dreadful chairs." She pointed to the old chairs opposite the couch. "Why don't we buy new ones? I've got that money Agatha left me. We can buy a couch the same size as this one so it matches, and a couple of armchairs."

Elsa-May dropped her head and frowned. "Those chairs are good. There's nothing wrong with them, Ettie. I don't know what you're talking about. That would be wasteful. We'll just get Jeremiah to fix them up and strengthen them a little, so they don't creak."

Ettie laughed. "Wouldn't you like a couch to sit on like this one?"

"*Nee.* It's all right I suppose, but I'd fall asleep on it, and I'd never get any knitting done." Right then, Snowy came bounding back inside through the dog door. "Snowy, sit on your bed!"

Snowy stared into her face.

"Go to your bed!" Elsa-May said a little more firmly.

He walked over and lay down on the dog bed in the corner. Ettie watched on in amazement.

IT WAS the next day when they visited with Ava and tried to enlist her help with their plans.

"Ava I'm hoping you'll be able to help us." Ettie asked.

"Of course I will. What with?"

Elsa-May took over by saying, "The detective thinks that Josh is somehow involved with Margaret's murder."

"That's impossible. How could he be?"

"He's not saying exactly what he's got on him, but we have to prove that Josh didn't have anything to do with her death," Ettie said.

"And how do we do that exactly if we don't even know why the detective thinks he's involved?" Ava asked.

"The thing is, the detective thinks Josh knows something that he's not saying, and that's as much as we know and probably that's all the detective knows too."

"Ettie and I are thinking because you're such good friends with Josh…"

"I'm not friends with Josh, but Jeremiah is."

"That's what Elsa-May meant; because your Jeremiah is such good friends with Josh perhaps Jeremiah could find out a few things?"

"Jeremiah would never get involved with anything like that. I know him, and he simply wouldn't do it."

Ettie's eyes twinkled. "That's why we have a plan."

"What plan? I'm not sure I like the sound of that." Ava took a deep breath. "Go on, what is it?"

"We thought if you could have Josh to dinner, you could steer the conversation toward Margaret and ask a few pointed questions that we'll give you," Elsa-May said.

"And then you want me to report back what he says?" Ava asked.

"Not quite," Ettie said.

"Nee, Ettie and I will be here listening in."

"At my *haus?* What, you mean you'll be hiding somewhere here in my *haus* to hear what Josh's answers are?"

Ettie nodded. "That's right. We'll be here to listen."

Ava shook her head. "Jeremiah would never allow it. He'd never approve of it."

Ettie continued, "That's what we thought, and that's why he would never have to know we were there."

"You want me to deceive my husband right after we've only just married?"

"Would it be easier to do after you've been married a few years?" Elsa-May asked.

Ava pressed a hand to her stomach. *"Nee,* Elsa-May. I would not want to do it now or in a few years. I never want to have to keep any secrets from Jeremiah. You're putting me in a bad spot."

"We're only asking because it will help Josh. If we can find out what he's keeping from the detective that will make the detective see he's not guilty of anything and Detective Kelly can find the real killer."

Ettie's mouth turned down at the corners. "For all we know, Margaret's murderer could be planning another murder as we're talking."

Ava shook her head. "I hate these types of situations. On the one hand I'll be helping Josh but on the other hand, I'll be keeping a secret from Jeremiah. I don't know what to do."

"We see no other way to do it, do we, Ettie?"

"Nee, we don't. We've thought it all through. We've talked to him twice, and we know he's not saying everything and the detective's talked to him and for some reason the detective thinks he knows more."

"And we didn't even tell Detective Kelly that's what we thought," Elsa-May added.

"I understand what you're saying, but can't we leave Jeremiah out of it? Isn't there some other way?"

"If there was another way we would've thought of it by now," Ettie said.

Ava groaned loudly.

"Since Jeremiah is my *grosskin* I know him pretty well, and I don't think he will mind if he happens to find out. After all, we're only doing it to help Josh," Elsa-May said.

"Elsa-May will take all the blame if Jeremiah finds out. I'll say I was there when Elsa-May left you with no other choice."

"Can I tell Jeremiah what happened after the dinner? That won't be deceiving him or keeping secrets on purpose, I suppose," Ava said.

"Jah that's right," said Elsa-May, "and put the blame on me just like Ettie said. I'll tell Jeremiah we forced you to do it."

"And Jeremiah knows what we're like, so he'll believe it," Ettie added.

After Ava breathed out heavily again, she said, "If you both think it's really necessary to help Josh then I'll do it. I'll invite Josh to dinner very soon, and I'll let you know when he's coming."

"Good and we'll get here early to hide before Josh gets here," Ettie said.

"And before Jeremiah gets home."

Ava heaved a sigh of reluctance and then nodded.

CHAPTER 14

"WHY DO you have to bring Snowy with you? It's going to be that much harder for us to hide," Ettie said to Elsa-May in the taxi on the way to Ava's house.

"I just don't like leaving him alone too much. He's only a small dog; he's more of a person really. Snowy can hide with us since he's only small."

"He's hardly ever alone. We're mostly home; we rarely go out."

"All the same, if we're only going to be hiding over there listening, I'm going to bring Snowy. There's no harm in that. No one minds a small dog around." Elsa-May leaned over to the driver, and asked, "You don't mind a small dog in your taxi, do you?"

"They're generally less problem than children. I don't mind a small dog as long as he stays in your lap."

"See, Ettie? The driver doesn't mind Snowy and neither will Ava mind."

"Well, all I can say is that I hope Snowy gets along with Jeremiah's dogs."

"Snowy likes other dogs."

"It wasn't Snowy I was thinking about. Snowy would make a tasty snack for Jeremiah's two big dogs."

Elsa-May looked worried. "I didn't think of that."

"That's obvious. You also haven't thought that his dogs will alert Jeremiah to our presence. He could bring the whole plan down around us."

"Should we turn around and leave him at home?"

Ettie shook her head. "It's too late now."

"Well, if it's too late to leave him home, stop complaining about it. You're always finding things to grumble about these days, Ettie."

Ettie pointed to herself. "Me?"

Elsa-May nodded.

"I don't see that's true. I generally keep quiet about all the things you do that annoy me."

Elsa-May's mouth fell open. "What could I possibly do that would annoy you?"

Ettie stared at Elsa-May. "I wouldn't know where to start. There's a long list of things you do that annoy me."

"Name one of them."

"The way you slurp your tea and your soup."

"You were the one that started the slurping. You used to do it all the time. When I started doing it, I was only imitating you. Then I enjoyed slurping."

"I stopped because you complained; now I see how irritating it is."

"You're being petty-minded. Do you have any real complaints?"

"The way you clang your spoon on the bottom of the soup plate with every mouthful you take. The way you leave the cupboard doors open continually, and you never push your chair in when you leave the table. You also leave the suds in the bottom of the kitchen sink after you do the dishes."

"What's wrong with leaving the suds in the sink, Ettie?"

"It looks untidy, and I like a clean and tidy, dry sink."

Elsa-May screwed up her nose. "Sinks weren't made to be dry. Well, I didn't know I did so much to annoy you. Maybe we should rethink our living arrangements."

"Here we are, ladies," the taxi driver said as he pulled up outside Jeremiah's house.

The two sisters and Snowy got out of the taxi, and as the taxi was driving away, Ettie said, "I'm sure I do things that annoy you as well."

"And I tell you about them straight away. I don't store them all up to tell you all your annoying habits all at once."

"Would you rather me tell you as soon as you do something that annoys me?"

Elsa-May said, "Let's talk about this at another time. Let's just get through the night and see if we can help Josh."

"I agree with that; good idea." Ettie regretted saying anything to Elsa-May. Now her feelings were hurt, and Ettie knew at some stage that she'd have to be the one to apologize.

Ava opened the door to them. "Hurry up. Jeremiah could be home soon, and I don't need him to see you." Her eyes fell to the bundle in Elsa-May's arms. "You brought Snowy?"

"I'm not saying a word," Ettie said as she walked past Ava into the house.

"He's only a small dog. He can hide with us in the utility room. I've been thinking that would be the best place for us to stay. It's just off from the kitchen, and Jeremiah wouldn't go in there. He wouldn't, would he?"

"Nee, he never goes in there. I think that's a good place to stay. Snowy won't bark or anything, will he?"

"Nee; he's not a barker at all." Elsa-May walked past Ava into the house.

Ava closed the door behind them. "We might as well get everything ready. I've nearly finished dinner. I just need to set the table. I've cooked enough dinner for both of you, and I can give Snowy some of the other dogs' food."

"We've been worried about Jeremiah's dogs knowing that Snowy's here," Ettie asked.

"Where are Jeremiah's dogs?" Elsa-May asked.

"He took them with him today. He often takes them to work, and they stay on the back of the wagon. Or sometimes they wander around where he's working."

"We're worried about when the dogs come home; they might know there's another dog here and bark or something. I quite forgot about his dogs when I decided to bring Snowy."

"Nee, it should be all right because he puts them in the barn at night. He used to leave them out, but they were blamed for killing chickens, so now he locks them in every night so they won't be accused of killing livestock when it's actually a fox or something."

"Ah, that's good to put them in the barn."

"What time have you got Josh coming?"

"He'll most likely be coming soon; that's why I'm so glad that you arrived when you did."

"We'll help you set the table. I will while Elsa-May looks after Snowy."

"*Denke.* Jeremiah and I have been meaning to get a second table for the dining room so we can have our main meals in the dining room and have breakfast in the kitchen where it's more cozy."

While Ettie and Ava set the table, Ettie drilled Ava on the questions she was to ask Josh. Elsa-May was making a comfortable place for Snowy on the blanket she'd brought with her.

"I can hear hoofbeats." Ava looked out the kitchen window. "Here comes Jeremiah now and Josh is right behind him."

Ettie hurried into the utility room then stuck her head back into the kitchen. "Now, don't worry about feeding us," Ettie said, "We'll get something to eat later."

"Do you remember what questions you have to ask?"

"I do. It's all up here." Ava tapped her head.

"*Wunderbaar.*"

CHAPTER 15

AFTER TENDING TO THEIR HORSES, Josh and Jeremiah walked through the front door. From the utility room, the sisters heard only mumbles. They couldn't hear any words clearly.

"When they're having dinner in the dining room, we can move into the kitchen so we can hear better," Ettie whispered.

"That sounds like the best idea," Elsa-May agreed.

After the men had washed up, they sat down at the dinner table. Ava carried bowls of food out and set them in the center of the table. When the elderly sisters didn't hear anything they knew that were saying the silent prayer of thanks for the food.

"Okay let's go out now and listen in," Ettie said. "Shut the door quietly behind you so Snowy doesn't get out."

"Okay. You go first."

Ettie walked into the kitchen and was glad to see that the door leading to the dining room was closed. She crept out further and put her ear to the door. Soon she was joined by Elsa-May. They could only hear what was said when they had their ears to the door.

After some small talk, Ava started on the topic of Margaret Yoder.

"I was so sorry to hear about Margaret Yoder, Josh. I know she was once very important to you."

There was a moment of silence. "*Denke*, Ava. I suppose Jeremiah told you that we were going to get married at one point, but it never happened."

"*Jah*. I went to her funeral with Ettie and Elsa-May."

"I know. I saw you all there."

"You went too?" Jeremiah asked Josh in surprise.

"I didn't go to the service. I went to the graveyard and watched them place her in the ground. I saw that man she nearly married."

"That must've been very upsetting for you," Ava said.

"I don't know that she was going through with it anyway."

"You mean with her wedding?" Ava asked.

He nodded. "He was involved in some shady business, and she wasn't happy about it. I can't see she would've married the man."

"What's he doing—illegal things or something?" Ava asked.

Jeremiah butted in, "I'm sure Josh doesn't want to talk about things like this, Ava."

"*Nee*, it's alright. He gave her a ring that was worth a lot of money and then he wanted her to pretend to lose it or pretend to have it stolen so he could collect the insurance money."

"How does that work?" Ava asked. "Had he insured it

for more than what he paid for it? Otherwise, it wouldn't make sense."

"The thing was… and keep this to yourselves because the detective's been asking a lot of questions and I don't think it's anyone's business to know what was going on in Margaret's life. The man wanted Margaret to say that the ring was stolen or lost when the ring wouldn't have been at all."

"That's interesting. So then he would get all the money that the ring was worth, and he'd still have the ring itself?"

He nodded. "Correct, but Margaret refused to do it. She said she was never a dishonest person, and she wasn't going to start being dishonest just because she'd left the community."

"And you talked about things like this when you met with her?"

"We did talk about that and a lot of other things. He's not a good man."

Ava said, "Why can't you tell the detective that? It's nothing really private to do with Margaret and her life; it's about what the man tried to make her do."

"I'm not comfortable discussing Margaret with people I don't know very well."

Ettie and Elsa-May heard the ringing of cutlery against the plates while they ate.

"Is that annoying you, Ettie, hearing the clanging of the cutlery?"

"Sh." Ettie elbowed Elsa-May. "They'll hear you."

The conversation changed to other subjects. After a while, Ava said, "I'll take up these plates, and then bring the dessert out."

"I'll help with the plates," Jeremiah said as he pushed out his chair.

"Nee! You stay right there and talk to Josh; I can do it. I don't need any help tonight."

When they heard her on the way into the kitchen, Elsa-May and Ettie hurried back into the utility room just in case Jeremiah decided to help her anyway.

"Did you hear all that?" Ava asked when she opened the utility room door a little.

"We certainly did," Ettie whispered back. "Sounds like Cartwright is crooked just like Josh told us at the start."

"Good work, Ava. That's what we wanted to know. That's what he was keeping from us all along," Elsa-May said.

"And from the detective," Ettie added.

"I had better go take this dessert out to them now. I've got dinner still in the saucepan over there if you want to help yourselves while we're eating dessert."

Ettie said, "We'll stay in here to be certain not to be seen. After dinner, just put the men in the living room and then go out to the barn and call us a taxi. Have the taxi pick us up down the road on the corner outside the old red barn. We'll start walking as soon as you go outside."

"Okay." Ava nodded before she closed the door.

"The food smells delicious, and I'm getting quite hungry. I'll just go and get a little of something. Do you want some too?" Ettie asked.

"I'm hungry as well; we should get something to eat. Stay here; I'll go and get us something." Elsa-May opened the door as she went to walk past Ettie, and then Snowy raced through their legs.

They followed him trying to grab him, but he scampered through the door.

Ettie raced back into the utility room with Elsa-May not far behind her. By this time, the door of the kitchen had been pushed wide open.

"How did you let that happen, Ettie?"

"Me? You shouldn't have brought him. He's going to ruin everything."

"What do we do now?"

"Just wait here and be quiet," Ettie said.

"And what's this?" they heard Jeremiah say.

Then Ava said, "I forgot to tell you we're looking after Elsa-May's dog tonight."

"We are? Where has he been?"

"He's been sleeping in the utility room."

"Is Elsa-May all right?"

"She's quite all right. Well, the thing is, she asked me if I wanted to take the dog because it's too much work for her. I thought we could take him for a day or two to see how he fits in with us."

"When were you going to let me know about this?"

"I just forgot to mention it."

"He's very cute," Josh said.

"*Jah.* He is cute," Jeremiah admitted, "but we've already got two dogs, Ava. I definitely don't need another."

CHAPTER 16

WHEN JOSH WENT HOME LATER that evening, Ava carried the dishes to the sink while Jeremiah flung open the door to the utility room.

He stood looking at them with his arms folded. "I thought as much when I saw the pup. What are you two doing in here?"

"We didn't want to let Josh know that we were here."

He shook his head. "He's well and truly gone now. I'll take you both home, and the dog. I can only guess what you're doing in here." Jeremiah walked away.

"I think I've just been reprimanded by my grandson."

"I think you were." Ettie laughed quietly. "At least we have a way of getting home now."

They stepped into the kitchen not expecting to see Jeremiah, but there he was in front of them looking none too pleased.

He folded his arms. "I suppose you had Ava ask questions for you so you could hear the answers?"

"We only had the very best intentions. He's fallen

under suspicion of being guilty of something. That's what the detective told us."

"We were only trying to protect him," Ettie said.

"He was keeping something from us, and thanks to Ava, we've now found out about the fraud that Norman Cartwright was trying to commit. A million dollars worth."

"That's a lot of money," Ettie added.

"It's not right what happened here tonight. We've betrayed Josh's trust," Jeremiah said.

"*Nee*, not you—we have," Ettie said.

"Now we can tell the detective about the way the man wanted to defraud the insurance company. The detective wouldn't have stopped until he found out what Josh was hiding."

"We talked Ava into doing this for us. It's not her fault. She didn't want to do it," Ettie said.

"But she did want to help Josh, and that's the only reason she did this."

"I was going to tell you about it afterward, Jeremiah," Ava said.

"That would've been too late." His eye was caught by something on the floor. "What is that puddle on the floor over there?"

Elsa-May walked a few steps to have a closer look at what he was pointing at. "*Ach nee.* I'm sorry. I should've taken Snowy outside before now."

Ettie remained silent while trying not to laugh. She was tempted to say that it might have been better not to bring the dog, but there was no point in repeating what she'd already said. Elsa-May was already upset with her.

"I'm sorry, Ava and Jeremiah. I'll take him outside. Where's that leash?"

"It's in the utility room," Ettie said.

"You allowed the dog in the utility room where we store our food?" Jeremiah looked at Ava.

"The dog's only small, Jeremiah, and he was nowhere near the food," Ava said while she patted Jeremiah's arm.

"We should go now, Elsa-May."

"I'll clean the mess up before we go."

"I'll go hitch the buggy," Jeremiah said.

"Nee, we'll get a taxi. We don't want to cause you any trouble, Jeremiah. We've already been enough trouble for one evening," Ettie said.

"You have, there's no doubt about that. Nevertheless, I'll take you home anyway. No arguments; I'll go and hitch the buggy now." Jeremiah strode out of the room.

"I'm sorry, Ava, we didn't mean to put you in an awkward position like that," Ettie said.

"Well, that's what I was afraid of. He'll calm down but it might take him a bit of time. I'll get a mop and clean that."

"Nee, Ava, I'll do it," Elsa-May said.

"I will," said Ettie. "You hold the culprit, Elsa-May, and I'll get the mop."

Once Ettie had cleaned up the mess, she sat in the kitchen. The night had been problematic, but at least they had information, which would put Josh in a better light with the police. She only wished that they could have done this without involving Jeremiah and Ava.

On the way home, Ettie waited for Elsa-May to say something to calm Jeremiah.

Elsa-May finally spoke, "Please don't blame Ava for anything that happened tonight. She didn't even want to do it. It was all my idea."

"And mine too," Ettie said. "She was against the idea, and we talked her into it."

"I know this was not her doing. I must say I'm quite surprised that Ava hid it all from me."

"Ava was going to tell you when the night was over. She said she'd only do it if she could tell you about it, so she wasn't keeping anything from you."

"She is a very good honest girl."

He sighed deeply. "I know she is, but I just don't like things going on in my house that I have no idea of. You can't do anything like this again. I know you feel involved because this happened at your *haus* Ettie, but can you leave Ava out of things?"

"We will."

"Yes, we will. And we shouldn't have done it. If we knew that things would've turned out like this, I wouldn't have done it. Will you accept our apology?"

"*Jah.* Let's just pretend this whole thing never happened."

WHEN THEY FINALLY REACHED THEIR home, Elsa-May put Snowy down on the floor, and he walked out the dog door.

"I'll get us something to eat, Ettie. We've got some cold cuts, and I'll put something together quickly."

"Denke, sounds good." Ettie followed Elsa-May into the kitchen. "What a dreadful, dreadful night we've had."

"We reached our goal. We found out what we wanted, but at what cost?"

"We've caused trouble between two of our favorite people. And they're only newly married."

"I feel awful about it," Elsa-May said.

"Why does good come with bad sometimes?"

Elsa-May sighed. "Don't ask difficult things so late at night. Ava and Jeremiah are in love; nothing will affect that."

"I suppose so. It was a shock about the insurance and Cartwright trying to make her commit insurance fraud."

"Jah, that was a big shock."

"I didn't expect to find anything out like that."

"When should we tell the detective? I think that we should inform him as soon as possible," Elsa-May said.

"Jah, in the morning first thing."

CHAPTER 17

"You've got something to tell me?" Detective Kelly asked them the next morning when they were sitting across from him in his office.

"Yes, we do. We overheard Josh, the man that Margaret was once going to marry, telling someone that Norman Cartwright wanted her to pretend her ring was either lost or stolen so he could collect an insurance payout."

"Really? Margaret told someone that?"

"Yes, she did. Margaret was so upset she called Josh to talk about it. She didn't want to do it and told Norman she wouldn't. I think she had second thoughts about the marriage."

"Yes, that's the way it sounded. The way he told it," Elsa-May said.

"That is interesting. Fascinating," Detective Kelly said.

"Josh doesn't know we overheard what he said. He told Ava and Jeremiah that in confidence."

The detective frowned. "How did you happen to over-hear it?"

"Does that matter?"

The detective looked shocked at Ettie's reply.

Elsa-May butted in by saying, "We overheard it while Josh was having dinner at Ava and Jeremiah's place."

"You weren't also having dinner there?"

"We were at their house, but Josh didn't know we were there."

"Sounds like that's all I need to know." The detective had smirked before he leaned back in his chair. "I think I'll have to take a little more interest in the motives of Norman Cartwright in all this. Did you hear if she shared anything else with Josh?"

"No. That's all. Do you think there's more?"

He folded his arms across his chest. "I don't know."

"What about Norman's daughter?" Ettie asked.

"That's another matter entirely. We have DNA that was found at the scene of the crime."

"How so?" Elsa-May asked.

"Where?" Ettie asked.

"We found her DNA under Margaret's fingernails, but Paisley has a solid alibi. So we're still looking into that."

"Detective, you led us to believe you thought Josh was guilty of something."

"I'm sorry, I know I did, but it was important that you get the information for me to find out how much Josh knows. He could be in danger."

"How can we believe that? If you keep hiding the truth about things from us?" Elsa-May clasped her hands in her lap.

"I'll get to that later. Paisley had a reasonable explanation why her DNA was found under Margaret's fingernails. She told us that she and Margaret had a physical altercation wherein Margaret scratched her on the arm. She even showed us the marks left by Margaret."

"That's hard to believe. I'd say Margaret was defending herself."

"Is there any way to tell if the scratches happened the day Margaret was murdered or the day before?"

"I don't think so. The scratches didn't draw blood; they were more like scrapes really. Just enough for DNA to be found under her fingernails the next day."

"Could Paisley have slipped away from the place where she had the alibi?" Elsa-May asked.

He shook his head. "It was too far away for that. She wouldn't have been able to get out and get back. There were too many witnesses at the function where she was. Paisley was quite cooperative and even offered to undergo a lie detector test."

"I would have thought that DNA under a victim's fingernails would be proof enough but on the other hand, you say her alibi is solid."

"What she told us checks out. The other thing was there didn't seem to be signs of a struggle at the scene; everything was quite orderly except the book that was dropped."

"Can you say that there were no signs of a struggle? What signs would there be out in the open? It wasn't as though they were in a house where furniture would've been knocked over."

"No, Elsa-May, but the medical examiner didn't find bruises consistent with a struggle."

"So from her altercation where Paisley was scratched there must've been no bruises from that?"

"No; none. The coroner is suggesting she might have been under the influence of a drug when she was killed, which is why there were no signs of a struggle. What normally happens during strangulation is that the victim's clothing will get caught in whatever the victim is being strangled with and provide marks, or the victim will try to scratch the assailant. None of the usual signs were present."

"That's interesting."

"I'm probably not doing a good job explaining all this."

"You are. It's just that all this is new to us."

"Since there were none of the usual signs there is every possibility that the woman was given some kind of drug beforehand. The other thing was, the angle of the marks on her neck suggest that she was strangled by someone tall."

"Or could she have been on her knees at the time? I noticed her knees were red," Ettie said.

"Yes, there was mention of that in the autopsy, which might fall in line with her being drugged beforehand as well. She could have fallen to her knees feeling unwell, and then her assailant took the opportunity to step in and strangle her."

"Why does it take so long for the toxicology report to come back? It's frustrating waiting so long," Ettie said.

"There's every possibility that several laboratories are involved. If there are two or more toxins found in her body that also slows things up beyond the time that I estimated."

Elsa-May shook her head.

"I know this is frustrating, but sometimes we just have to be patient and wait. There's quite a lot of waiting in my job. It would help if I could find out more from Josh Tomson about Norman Cartwright's insurance fraud plans. I need to know exactly how much Josh Tomson knows."

"You could try to talk to him again yourself. Tell him you heard rumors that he met with Margaret," Ettie suggested to the detective. "I think he needs the right motivation. He wouldn't want there to be a cloud hanging over Margaret's reputation. So if he thought by giving you the information he was clearing Margaret's name, then he just might tell you what you want to know."

"Good thinking, Ettie. I agree." Elsa-May looked over at Kelly. "I do believe Ettie's right. He'll talk to you if you put that line of thinking across to him."

"I've not got anything to lose by trying. Thanks for the hot tip, Ettie. Are you sure that Josh didn't mention anything else?"

"Like what?" Elsa-May asked.

"Anything at all?"

Ettie and Elsa-May looked at each other and then looked back at the detective. "No, nothing." It was then that Ettie noticed something different about his office. It was a different color. "Have you redecorated?"

"I have. What do you think of it?"

"I think that it looks more inviting. The cream looks softer than the steely gray. And you've got new filing cabinets. I don't know why I didn't notice it when I first came in."

"Couldn't you smell the new paint?" he asked.

Ettie shook her head. "Not with my sinuses the way they are at the moment."

"I can smell the paint just slightly now that you've mentioned it," Elsa-May said. "Are you keeping this old desk?" Elsa-May patted the heavily scratched teakwood desk.

"It has history, and it's a good size. I was going to update it, but I decided to keep it."

"Getting back to this whole thing with Margaret. You said, or you hinted at, there being something more you were going to tell us after we spoke with Josh the second time around," Ettie said.

"I might as well tell you, but you have to swear you'll keep it strictly between the two of you. If it gets out, it's going to ruin our whole investigation, threaten my job here, and possibly endanger Josh, and Margaret's Amish family."

"Now you have to tell us," Elsa-May said.

"We'll be sure to keep it to ourselves, whatever it is."

The detective let out a deep breath. "Margaret Yoder was one of our own."

"One of your own? What does that mean?" Elsa-May asked.

"She was a police officer."

Ettie gasped. "No!"

"Yes! She was. As soon as she went through the academy, she went straight into special operations."

"You mean undercover work?" Elsa-May asked.

"That's correct."

Ettie and Elsa-May stared at one another.

The detective went on to say, "If Josh knows she was working undercover it might ruin everything. That's why I've been trying to have you find out whether Josh knows, without letting you two know, that Margaret was under-cover. Hopefully, she hasn't told him that she was working for us."

Ettie and Elsa-May looked at each other with raised eyebrows.

"No one in the community knew she was in the police force. It would be a surprise to everybody."

"She was a da … I mean she was a very good one, too," the detective stated. "Unless she's told someone she was working undercover."

"So she wasn't really genuinely engaged to Norman, she was investigating him?" Ettie asked.

"That's right. We've been after him for some time. She was gathering information about him. She's already gath-ered enough information to put him away for years, but we're always after more. We were hoping to cast a wide net to see who else we could nab."

"You think someone found out she was a detective, and that's why she was killed?" Elsa-May asked.

"That's exactly what I'm trying to find out. She could've been killed for the diamond she was wearing. Alternatively, Norman might have killed two birds with the one stone, so to speak. He could have done away with her, and been able to report the diamond stolen at the same time."

"Couldn't you get a search warrant to see if he's got the diamond hidden somewhere?" Ettie asked.

"We could, but we're holding off. We're trying to get him for nearly a million dollars worth of insurance fraud."

"How long has she been a police officer?" Elsa-May inquired.

"She left your community and went straight into the police force."

"Why was she using her own name if she was undercover?" Elsa-May asked.

"She's had various names for undercover operations she did with us, but when we decided to set up Norman Cartwright, we thought it fitting to use her own identity since she'd truly left the Amish. She was no longer in contact with her own family or former friends, and we thought a former Amish woman trying to make it on her own would've appealed to Cartwright. And we were right."

"Still seems odd to me," Elsa-May huffed.

"Nevertheless, it worked. Cartwright immediately fell in love. He tried to better her position in life and got her an internship with a local real estate agency."

"And it was Brandy who thought to change her name to make her sound more like a realtor and less Amish. She told us so herself. Brandy changed her own name."

"She told us that the name of Margo Rivers would be more in line with the real estate job."

"Brandy changed her own name you say?" the detective asked.

"Yes. She said she changed it years ago to fit better on her business card."

The detective leaned back in his chair. "Do you happen to know her former name?"

The sisters exchanged glances.

"What was it, Ettie?"

"It was Boadicea. That was her first name."

"That's right it was. I remember her saying she didn't like the name. Wasn't her last name really long?"

"Yes, it was long. Was it Winchester or something like that?"

"Quite possibly," Elsa-May answered. "Yes. I'm certain it was Winchester because that's how she decided on the last name of 'Winnie.'"

They looked back at the detective.

"Do you suspect Brandy of something?" Elsa-May asked.

"Only of being too attractive." He laughed. "But we can't arrest people for that. I'm sorry; it was a bad joke. No. I just like to know who I'm dealing with in an investigation like this. I've got to look at everyone surrounding the victim."

"Would you have access to look that up from her social security number or something?"

"Yes, and now that I know, I'll look into it further."

"Well this is a shock," Elsa-May said cradling her head in her hands. "We never guessed that Margaret was an officer."

"If Josh knew the truth he seems to be keeping it to himself. The most he told Jeremiah was that Norman Cartwright was not an honest man."

"It's hard to know if Margaret confided in him fully," the detective commented. "Over the last few months, her phone calls and visits with Josh were more frequent, which was concerning to us."

"You were having her followed?"

"This is a delicate operation. We had to be sure we had the right person in the right job. She was crucial to us since she'd become so close with Norman. We couldn't just pluck another woman like her from our force to take her place."

"Where do you go from here with your investigation, Detective?" Elsa-May asked.

"We're still following a multitude of leads. And if you ladies will excuse me I'd better get back to it."

CHAPTER 18

ETTIE AND ELSA-MAY left the police station feeling stunned. The detective had offered that someone would drive them home, but they preferred to delay going home. Instead, they went for a walk up the street and then they'd get a taxi home.

"That's left me in shock, Elsa-May."

"Me too. I never would've guessed she was a police officer, an undercover one at that."

"I wonder if she was still in love with Josh and that's why she met with him. Maybe she just gave the hint to him that the wedding to Norman wasn't going to go ahead."

"You think she might have had second thoughts on leaving him and the community?"

"She was bound to have had second thoughts from time to time. I know I've often looked back over my life and wondered what would have happened if I'd made different decisions."

"Let's find a café and have a cup of tea and something to eat before we go home. I feel like we deserve a treat."

"That sounds good, Ettie. There are some cafes three blocks up this way."

They walked to the café in silence and were pleased to find one with a large display of cakes. After gazing into the cabinet at the cakes and tasty treats, they placed their order. It was a pot of tea for two, a ginger cake for Ettie, and a lemon slice for Elsa-May. Being three in the afternoon, the café was close to empty; they chose a table near the window.

"She must've felt that being a police officer was her calling in life. So much so that she left all of her old life behind her—Josh, the community, and her family."

"Going by what the detective said, she was very good at what she did."

"Nothing is worth a life like that, though."

"*Nee* and nothing is worth leaving the community for. But in her mind, she would have been doing the right thing, and that was her choice to make."

When their number was called out, Elsa-May got up and brought the tea and food back to the table.

Ettie took a bite of the ginger cake. "Mmm. I needed this. I'm quite hungry."

"Me too, but I'm always hungry." Elsa-May chortled. "Do you think I'm a bit thinner since I've been walking?"

Ettie stared at Elsa-May as she munched on a large mouthful of cake. "*Jah*, I think you could possibly be a bit thinner."

Elsa-May swallowed her mouthful. "That sounds a bit doubtful. I don't mind if I haven't lost weight. I won't be upset. Just tell me what you think. The doctor said I was too heavy and needed to lose weight, and that's why I've been walking. Surely I would've lost a lot by now."

"Maybe as well as walking you should eat less—just a little less?"

"The doctor didn't say that, did he?"

"*Nee,* not that I recall, but it does make sense."

"Forget I asked anything. Do you think Josh knew what Margaret was doing? Seems that if he did know he's keeping it to himself."

Ettie was relieved she didn't have to answer any more questions about her sister's size. "Well if she was such a good undercover agent she wouldn't have told anyone."

"That's true; she would've had to make a solemn declaration, or something along those lines, that she wouldn't divulge what she was up to. I'm certain she would've stayed true to that."

"I don't think she was in touch with Josh right after she left. It seemed to be in the last year or so, most likely when she got involved with Norman."

"What if she only wanted Josh to know she wasn't really in love with Norman?"

"Are you thinking that she might still have been in love with Josh? What if she still wanted Josh but didn't want to stay in the community. Or what if she was in love with him and was thinking of coming back?"

"We'll never know. I wonder how long the Police Academy goes for their training?"

"That's a good question, Elsa-May, maybe it goes for a year. I'm just guessing that. Something in the back of my mind tells me the training goes for a year. Shall we go to the library after this and look it up?"

"We could just ask the detective next time we see him. But we could go to the library, and while we're there, we could look up a few other things too. We can see what we can find out about Paisley, and Norman Cartwright."

"I'm sure you won't find anything else that the police don't already know. They would have accessed all the public records by now."

"You never know, there might be something they've missed. They're not infallible you know."

Ettie finished her last mouthful of ginger cake. "I'm going to try to make my own ginger cake when this is all over. It's really tasty and satisfying."

"Do you think it was mean of the detective not telling us straightaway about Margaret?"

"I do. What purpose did he have keeping a secret from us?" Ettie used a paper napkin to dab at the cake crumbs on the corners of her mouth.

"He could've told us from the beginning. We're keeping his secret now just as easily as we could've kept it then."

"It's strange that she had a kind of fake life that was made up. She wasn't in love with Norman, and she had to pretend to be. Not even Brandy knows about the whole thing. Maybe it is just us who know unless Margaret told Josh or someone else."

"We likely won't find out until they find Margaret's killer."

"We don't know much about Paisley either. Except

that she didn't like Margaret. I don't believe Margaret started that fight."

"Neither do I. She must've started it, and Margaret was trying to defend herself; that's why Margaret would've scratched Paisley. Sounds like it might have been an accidental scrape too, and not a real fight."

"We do know she worked in her father's business and grew up with her mother, but that's all. That, and she never seems to smile, and she's a smoker."

"We've only seen her at the funeral, and not many people smile at funerals."

"I suppose that's true, but she had a surly-looking face."

"Come on finish up your tea so we can go to the library."

LATER THAT AFTERNOON, they settled behind the last available computer in the library.

"I've never seen it so crowded in here before, Ettie."

"I think it's school break or some such thing."

"Ah, that's right. I think it is. What shall we look up first?"

"We just found everything out about Margaret, so there's no need to look her up. I just had a thought; I hope Detective Kelly doesn't still think that Josh killed Margaret in a jealous rage."

"I wouldn't think so. He never said anything like it, did he?"

"*Jah,* he did, but I'm hoping he's changed his mind.

Don't forget how he's not straightforward and honest with us; not like Detective Crowley used to be."

"Speaking of Detective Crowley, Kelly didn't mention that Crowley had called in on him."

"I wonder what he'd make of all this latest information."

"We can't tell him."

"What if he already knows? Crowley could already know that Margaret was undercover. Maybe he was only there to get information from us to see how much we knew about Margaret."

"You might be right. And remember, he did ask us what else we'd been told about Margaret?"

"*Jah!* And I thought nothing of it at the time."

"Kelly seemed particularly interested in the fact that Brandy had changed her name."

"Do you want to see what we can find out about her too?"

"*Jah.* Why don't we start with Norman Cartwright?"

"Please yourself."

"We're looking for anything that might be of interest. I don't know exactly what to look for. Just keep scrolling through all the things about him and see what we can find."

After a few general news items on Norman, they found a picture of Norman with Brandy.

"Why are they together? Does this mean anything, Ettie? They look good and cozy together."

"She did say that they were friends, and he puts business her way. It probably wouldn't be unusual for them to go to functions together."

"I suppose that's true, so that doesn't really tell us anything, but she seems to like him an awful lot, don't you think?"

"I noticed. I definitely think that she might like him as more than just a friend. She was looking around at the funeral for him, and she seemed a little put out that she was not going in the same car as him from the service to the graveyard. She was delegated to the other car, and Sarah and Ava went in the car with him, taking her place."

"I remember that."

"Do you think Brandy killed Margaret so she could marry Norman?"

"She could've been jealous, but I can't see that she would've killed over something like that. Brandy is an attractive woman so surely she could get any man she wanted—don't you think so?"

"Yes, I do agree. I would say Brandy could get any man she wanted given her looks and vibrant personality. But what if she couldn't? What if the very man she wanted was the only man who wasn't interested in her?"

"I'm just not feeling that she would be a killer. Just see what else we can find out from this box."

Ettie giggled. "Okay." Over the next hour, they found quite a few pictures of Brandy and Norman together. "There are a lot of pictures of the two of them together."

"Do you think that they had a romantic relationship before Margaret came along?"

"That seems a possibility going by what we've seen here."

"What about Ruth Fuller? Should we ask her what she knows about Brandy and her past relationships? She was the one who introduced us to Brandy so she could know more about her."

"According to Ruth, she's been a customer of Ruth's bakery for a very long time."

"We can go and visit Ruth tomorrow. Now let's see what we can find out about Paisley Cartwright." After trying a few different searches and spelling her first name in a few different ways, they still came up with nothing on Norman Cartwright's daughter."

"So there's nothing on here about her."

"*Nee* and that in itself is odd."

"What kind of thing were you hoping to find?"

"I don't know. I don't know what we're looking for until we see it."

They spent a while at the library before they went home, having also found nothing on a Boadicea Winchester.

CHAPTER 19

ETTIE AND ELSA-MAY walked into Ruth's bakery. The retail store was out in front of the massive bakery where thousands of loaves were made daily.

"You ask if Ruth's here," Elsa-May said to Ettie.

"She should be. She's always at work by this time."

"Can I help you?" A young man asked.

Ettie took a step forward. "Yes. I'm just wondering if Ruth would be here at the moment."

"Yes, she's here."

"Can we see her?"

"I'll get her. What's your name?"

"Tell her Ettie and Elsa-May are here."

"Okay." The young man was gone for several minutes, and when he came back, he said, "Come this way." He opened a half door, and they walked through to the back where Ruth's office was.

"It's nice to see you both. What brings you here today? I heard about the murder at your place, Ettie; it was in the newspaper. One of my workers told me about it. I didn't make it to the Sunday meeting just past because I had a burst pipe and the water was everywhere in here. It went right through everything, and we had to close down for two days."

"I'm sorry to hear that, Ruth. That must've been dreadful."

"We didn't know, or we would've come to help you clean," Elsa-May said.

"The insurance company paid for it all to be cleaned up. They were very good."

"We've come here to ask a question about Brandy."

"Sit." She pointed to two chairs.

When they were both seated, Ettie asked, "Did you know that Brandy's intern was Margaret Yoder?"

"Nee. I know she's got a few assistants and whatnot, but I've never met any of them. I've met Brandy and one of the men from her firm, but I don't know everyone who works there. She never mentioned to me that Margaret Yoder was working for her. Most likely because Margaret had already left the community and it was none of my business what she did."

"I suppose that does make sense. Brandy advised her she should change her name to Margo Rivers so nobody would know she was Amish, so I suppose she wouldn't go around blabbing that she had a former Amish person working for her."

"Do you know anything about Brandy's personal relationships?"

"I know she doesn't appear to have any. I've never seen with anybody and she's never spoken about anybody. I never thought to ask her. We don't have that kind of a relationship."

"*Denke*, Ruth."

"Why are you asking?"

"We're asking because she seems to have some fondness for Norman Cartwright.

"Oh, I know Norman."

"You do?"

"Yes, I do. When I was going through a rough patch recently, he offered to loan me money."

"How well do you know him?"

"I know he's in the habit of offering businesses short-term loans. I got the impression that he's not completely honest—that's why I told him I didn't need money. Mind you it would've come in handy at the time."

"Who told you he wasn't honest?"

"I don't remember exactly. Maybe it's just more of the impression that I've gotten about the man."

"That's interesting. *Denke*, Ruth, you've been a really good help."

"I don't see how. I haven't really said anything. I should've gone to the funeral—Margaret Yoder's, but I'm just so busy here all the time."

"Don't worry. No one else in the community went except Ettie, me, Sarah and Ava."

"No one else went?"

"Not even her parents, or her other siblings besides Sarah?" Ruth seemed surprised. "I would've thought that some of them would've gone. What about Josh Tomson? I hear that he was seen with her a couple of times recently.

I had hoped the girl would return to him. It would've made a nice romantic story."

"He did go to the cemetery. Do you remember who told you they were together?"

Ruth shook her head. *"Nee.* I talk to so many people every day I can't say. It was in the last few months. I can tell you that much." Ruth stared at the two sisters. "What are you trying to find out? I can do some asking around for you."

"Nee, we don't want to endanger you in any way. A murderer is still on the loose, and it might be dangerous to ask questions."

"I would just bring things up casually in conversation. Don't worry about me. I'm old enough to look after myself. Just tell me what you want me to find out," Ruth said.

"We really came here to find out what you know about Brandy and her relationships," Ettie asked.

"Jah. And particularly if she had once had a relationship with Norman Cartwright."

"I'll keep my ears open and let you know if I hear anything that I think might be helpful. What does your detective think about all this?

Ettie pushed her lips out. "He's not really sharing much with us."

"There is some talk about Norman's daughter not being happy about not having a full inheritance if her father were to remarry, so if you hear anything about her that might be helpful," Elsa-May said.

"I've heard about her, but I've never met her," Ruth said.

Ettie raised her eyebrows. "What have you heard?"

"Nothing really; I've just heard that she exists—that Norman has a daughter. Apart from that, I know nothing about her."

"*Denke,* Ruth, we won't hold you up anymore today. We'll just buy some bread and we'll be on our way."

"*Jah, denke* for your help," Elsa-May added. They made their way outside, and once they'd stepped onto the pavement, Elsa-May said, "That was a complete waste of time."

"We weren't to know that."

"We're getting nowhere with this whole thing. What we need to do is find out more about Paisley. Right now, though, we need to buy some food."

THE SISTERS WERE SURPRISED when they got out of the taxi at their house to find Ruth waiting for them in her buggy. She climbed down as they walked over to her.

"We didn't expect to see you here so soon," Ettie said.

"I thought it might be important to tell you that I heard Norman Cartwright was going out of the country."

"That *is* interesting. How did you hear that?" Elsa-May asked.

"I have a good friend, Ted; he has a candy and video rental store. Norman called Ted directly and told him to hold onto his loan repayments for a while until someone gets in contact with him. Ted has a loan with Norman. Anyway, Norman told Ted he was going overseas."

"I think we need to tell the detective that, don't you, Elsa-May?"

"Jah, quick," Elsa-May said.

"I'll call him now." Ettie walked as quickly as she could to the shanty at the end of the road, where they were able to make their phone calls. She got straight through to Detective Kelly and told him that she'd just heard Cartwright was planning a trip out of the country.

Ettie walked back to Elsa-May and Ruth. "I got through to him. We'll just have to see what happens now."

"I'm glad I was able to help out. I hope they find Margaret's killer. They don't think it's Norman Cartwright himself do they?" Ruth asked.

"I'm not certain, but from the sounds of it he hadn't told Kelly he was leaving the country. Kelly didn't sound happy."

"You'd think a bereaved man would want to stay put while the murder investigation of his fiancée was underway." Elsa-May slowly shook her head.

"Will you come inside, Ruth? Stay for dinner with us."

"Nee, denke. I'm tired, and I should get home. Another time perhaps?"

"I hope so; we don't see enough of you," Ettie said.

The two sisters walked inside after Ruth drove away.

Elsa-May said, "Cartwright leaving the country makes him look guilty."

"It certainly does. I suppose we'll just have to wait and see what happens next."

CHAPTER 20

THE NEXT DAY, Ettie and Elsa-May planned to go into the police station to find out what happened with Norman Cartwright, but their plans changed when Detective Kelly knocked on the door early in the day.

"Good morning, ladies," he said, as he walked through their front door.

"Good morning, Detective Kelly. Come in and take a seat."

"Did you manage to catch Norman before he flew out of the country?" Elsa-May asked.

"Thanks to the information you gave us, he was apprehended just before he boarded the plane. He was searched by the airport authorities, and the diamond that was allegedly stolen was located on his person."

"So he *was* committing insurance fraud?" Ettie asked.

"Yes and not only that, we enacted the warrants we had for his house, and we've taken dozens of boxes of documents back to the station. With the information that Margaret already gave us, we've got enough to send him away for tax evasion and now for fraud. At this stage, however, there's no evidence to suggest that he killed Margaret."

The detective's phone sounded from his pocket. He pulled it out and looked at it. "It's the station."

"Go ahead and answer it," Elsa-May said.

The ladies listened in.

"Yes, Steve? He's there now? What's he saying exactly?" The detective smiled and raised his eyebrows. "Did you tape his confession? Keep him right there in the interview room. I'll be there in fifteen." He ended his call.

"Good news, Detective?"

"Very good news. It seems that when the news of Norman Cartwright's arrest got out, it prompted someone to come forward with a confession."

"Who?" The elderly sisters asked at the same time.

"A man has come forward claiming that Cartwright paid him to hold Margaret up at gunpoint and steal her ring. He said he did as Cartwright told him, but the woman was very much alive when he left." He bounded to his feet. "Excuse me, ladies. I've got questions I'd like to ask him."

"Yes, of course, go," Ettie said.

When the detective left, Elsa-May and Ettie sat back down.

"What do you think about that? He paid someone to hold Margaret up at gunpoint. What a horrible thing to do to poor Margaret."

"Jah. That's a dreadful thing that he did."

"The man who has come forward must've been worried that Norman would pin the murder on him."

"The police were getting too close. If he hadn't made his confession now, it would've been worse for him when they caught up with him."

"It doesn't sound as though Norman killed her or wanted her dead because he could have had someone kill her and take the diamond at the same time."

"I hope the detective's suspicions don't fall back onto Josh."

"That's exactly what I'm afraid of."

"You know, Elsa-May, I have a feeling that Sarah might know more about things than she's letting on. Something made her go to the funeral in spite of her parents' decision. What if Margaret confided in her older *schweschder?*"

"You could be right, Ettie, and she was the only one from her entire *familye* to go to her funeral, so there was a bond there."

"Shall we visit her tomorrow to see what we can find out?"

"Sounds like the best thing to do."

AFTER ELSA-MAY and Ettie had knocked on Sarah's door, one of Sarah's young children answered.

"Hi, is your *mudder* home?" Elsa-May asked.

As the little girl nodded, Sarah appeared behind her daughter. "Elsa-May, Ettie, come inside; it's nice to see you."

"Denke, Sarah. We've come here to talk to you about Margaret." After she spoke, Ettie looked over to the living

room and saw Sarah's other two children sitting down and playing.

"Okay; we can talk in the kitchen. You go in there and sit down, and I'll be in as soon as I make sure we won't be interrupted."

Ettie and Elsa-May sat in the kitchen and waited for Sarah to get her children organized.

"They'll be quiet for a while now. Can I get you tea or *kaffe?*"

"*Nee,* just sit and talk to us."

When Sarah sat, Ettie began by saying, "Did Margaret tell you anything about her life?"

"What do you mean?"

"We might as well tell you that the man she was engaged to has been arrested under fraud and tax evasion charges. He was trying to commit insurance fraud with the ring he gave Margaret."

"Mr. Cartwright has been arrested?"

The sisters nodded.

"He seemed a nice man when I was speaking to him at her funeral. Have they found out who killed her yet?"

"*Nee,* they haven't. So, did Margaret tell you anything at all about Cartwright or why she was really with him?"

"I guess you know?"

"We might. Tell us what you know about her. What she told you about her life."

She sucked in her lips. "She told me things that I was to never tell anyone."

"About being undercover?"

"You *do* know!" Sarah gasped.

"*Jah,* but we weren't sure that you knew."

160

"She needed to talk to someone. She was under a great deal of stress. We met every couple of weeks down by the old mill house. She'd call me the day before from a pay phone, and I'd meet her there at a time she'd tell me. It was always a different time of day but always at the same place."

"Did she say she was in danger?"

"I think she always felt unsafe when she was with that man. It was hard to talk to Mr. Cartwright at Margaret's funeral, but I guessed that he was still under investigation, so I had to act as though I knew nothing—that's what she would've wanted."

"He's still under investigation, and no one else knows she was undercover so please still keep it quiet," Ettie said.

"I will. That's the life she chose. She didn't have to do it. I told her to leave the job. I didn't see that it was worth all the stress. I think she was considering it," Sarah said.

"The latest we heard from the detective was that someone came forward and admitted to taking the diamond from her outside my *haus,* but he said she was alive when he left her."

Elsa-May explained further, "We were there when the call came through to the detective. The man had given himself up when he heard that Norman Cartwright had been arrested."

"Margaret told me she'd been giving the police information on him. He was hiding money in overseas accounts and doing other illegal things. When she told me many of the things, I didn't really understand them. She only told me what she was doing because she knew that I wouldn't tell anyone."

"It was risky for her to meet with you."

"She said if Norman had her followed it was just her meeting up with her sister. The secrecy could be explained easily because our parents wouldn't have wanted me to be seeing her after she'd left the community."

"I suppose that's a point," Ettie said. "Is there anything else she said that might help us find who the killer is?"

"Shouldn't you leave that to the police?"

"Probably, but we feel involved—and responsible almost—because it happened on Ettie's property."

"Margaret was doing an open house for me," Ettie explained.

"I know that."

Elsa-May asked Sarah, "Does your mother know about the work Margaret was doing?"

"Only I knew. I haven't told *Mamm* anything, and my husband only knows that I met with her to keep in touch. He didn't like it, but he allowed me to do it."

"That's most likely best. Your sister was taking a big risk talking to you."

"Margaret didn't have many friends. She told me most of the other police are friends with each other, but she always felt she was an outsider; she never fitted in with them. It's a shame she had to die in the way she did, living a fake life with a fake name; living a life that should've belonged to someone else."

Ettie realized Sarah hadn't answered her previous question from moments ago. "Is there anything else important that you think we should know?"

"She said if anything happens to her she was ready for it."

"Sounds like she was half expecting something to happen to her."

"More than half expecting it I'd say."

"Sarah, if anything else comes to mind will you let us know?" Ettie asked.

"Jah, I will. I could think of something later. We had many talks."

"Would you speak with the detective and let him know what you told us?"

She breathed out heavily. "I will. If it helps find who killed her, I will."

"We'll go to the station now and tell him what you've told us," Ettie said, pushing herself up from the table.

"Denke, both of you. It's comforting to know that you two still care about her even though she left the community."

"We do care." Elsa-May stood up. "Now we'll leave you and your little ones alone."

"I'll walk you out."

CHAPTER 21

"Margaret told her sister she was undercover?" Detective Kelly asked as though he didn't want to believe it.

"Was she technically undercover if she was using her real personal identity—the one she was born with?"

The detective pulled a sour face. "No need to use semantics on me, Elsa-May. She was undercover and told people about the subjects under investigation. That's unprofessional. I can't say I'm happy about that."

"Margaret's dead so she wouldn't be overjoyed about that either," Elsa-May blurted out.

"Be that as it may, she wasn't the agent I thought she was."

"I don't think you should pass judgment on someone who gave up their life in the course of doing their job," Elsa-May stated.

"How much did she tell her sister?" he asked.

"Sarah said she'd speak to you. It's best you hear it straight from her. I don't think she knows that much," Ettie said.

"I don't know if it'll be necessary to speak to Sarah, now that we've had a positive ID on the likely killer."

"You have?" Ettie asked.

"Yes. Darren Broadfoot came forward and told us he was paid to steal the ring from Brandy's finger. When he was driving away in the car he stole to use for the robbery, he passed a buggy. That's when I had your Josh Tomson come in for a lineup and Broadfoot has positively identified Tomson as the man in the buggy."

"So what does that mean? Do you think Josh killed Margaret because the man who robbed Margaret was …?"

The detective cut across Ettie, "We've apprehended Josh, and he's already been questioned. He's sticking to the story that he saw Margaret outside the house, wanted to talk to her and she told him to go because she was in the middle of working. He only left when she promised to meet him the next day. The next day, she never showed."

"It sounds like he's telling you the truth."

"Even if he is telling the truth now, he's withheld vital information which is an obstruction of justice," the detective said.

"Is that why you're still holding him?"

"I'm entitled to hold him for twenty four hours without charging him. I'm holding him for as long as I can to see what else comes to light. Perhaps his memory might become clearer the longer he's here. I'll let him go in the morning."

"Can we see him?"

"He hasn't been co-operative," the detective said.

"Can we see him, then?" Ettie repeated.

"Very well I'll have someone take you to him. He might

suddenly remember something that he'll tell you." The detective picked up his phone, pressed some buttons, and requested that Officer Phillips take them to one of the holding cells.

Rather than talk to him in the cell itself like they'd expected, the officer sat the sisters in an interview room and brought Josh to them.

"Elsa-May, Ettie. Are they going to let me out of here?" Josh said as he sat at the table in front of them.

"I think so," Elsa-May said.

"The detective told us that you saw Margaret directly after she'd been robbed."

"Jah that's right. Margaret told me to go away, and she'd meet me later where we usually met. She'd already told me everything she'd been doing—working for the police and everything. Did you know about that?"

"Jah. But the detective doesn't want that to be common knowledge," Ettie said.

"Well, I haven't told anyone anything. I figured you two would have known by now. The detective seems to trust you. I think Margaret had a feeling her life was in danger."

"Why's that?"

"She told me she'd been working undercover on different cases for the past few years, but had never been as scared as she had working this case. Norman Cartwright is a dangerous man—that's what she said. And she said everyone around him hated her and didn't want them to be together."

Elsa-May leaned forward. "Like who?"

"The daughter, his ex-wife, and even his staff. I was

just glad that we were talking again even though she said she would never come back to the community. I was still hoping she'd change her mind."

"Did she say she thought someone might be trying to kill her?"

"She told me about the insurance scam, and that she feared for her life when she was wearing the ring. That's why she insisted on always wearing the fake ring and not the real one. As far as I see it, if someone thought the ring she was wearing was the real one, she would've been in just as much danger as if she was wearing the real one."

Elsa-May nodded. *"Jah*, you're quite right."

"What did she say about Norman's daughter, Paisley?"

"When her father wasn't around she constantly called Margaret a gold digger, and other names that I can't repeat. She told Margaret her father would wake up to her being after his money."

"Did anything give Margaret a reason to think that her life might be in danger or threatened by Paisley?" Ettie asked.

"Nee. If there were anything like that she certainly didn't tell me about it because I would've remembered something like that. When the police force first had her get friendly with Norman, she said she was stepping on someone's toes. She mentioned she felt extreme anger coming from a woman."

"Did she say who this woman was or mention a name?" Ettie asked.

"It was the woman she started working for, the one you were at the funeral with."

"You mean Brandy Winnie?"

"Yeah, that's the one. Seems she was on the verge of having a serious relationship with the man herself until Margaret showed up."

Elsa-May turned and stared at Ettie.

"Did she feel in danger from Brandy?" Ettie asked him.

He nodded. "I think so, and then there was the man's ex-wife who didn't want her daughter's inheritance to go to Margaret. Are you able to get me out of here?"

"We'll have a talk with the detective and see what his plans are. Do you need a lawyer?" Ettie asked.

He shrugged his shoulders. "I don't know. Did the detective say that you should have a lawyer? He asked me if I had one and I said no."

"We can find you one if you need one," Ettie assured him.

Elsa-May added, *"Jah,* if you're not out of here by tomorrow. I don't think he can hold you for too long unless you're charged with something. He said he'll let you out in the morning."

"Denke for coming to see me," Josh said. "Do you best to get me out of here."

When they were escorted out of the interview room, they waited again to talk to Detective Kelly.

Once they were sitting in his office across from him, he asked, "So what did he have to say?"

"He seems to think that Margaret felt threatened by Brandy," Ettie said.

"And also from Norman's ex-wife."

"I don't care what he thinks. All I care about was what Margaret said to him." The detective pressed his lips firmly together.

Ettie glanced over at Elsa-May, who looked a little shocked at Detective Kelly's outburst. Was it because they'd mentioned Brandy as perhaps being involved?

"Perhaps you should talk to him yourself, then. Ettie and I are only trying to help."

"Yes, I know, forgive me. But you're helping through the filtered view that Josh Tomson's not guilty."

Elsa-May shot back, "And you're looking at things as though he is guilty!"

Suddenly the detective leaped off his chair and stood. "If you ladies will excuse me I've got many things to do." He tapped on a huge file of folders on the side of his desk. "I have to personally go through all these phone records and text messages of Cartwright's."

Ettie wondered why he'd have to do that personally but with the mood he was in, she wasn't brave enough to ask. She pushed herself up, and as she did, Elsa-May also stood. "We'll wait to hear from you."

"Thank you for coming in. Do you need someone to drive you home?"

"No thank you," Elsa-May said before she turned and walked out the door followed closely by Ettie.

When they were clear of the station, Elsa-May said, "The man's just rude."

"Let's go home and try to forget about all this nasty business for a while."

CHAPTER 22

AFTER ETTIE and Elsa-May had finished breakfast the next day, they heard a knock on their door.

"Who could that be?" Ettie asked.

"Open the door and see. I'll hold Snowy back." Elsa-May took hold of Snowy, so he wouldn't jump all over the person at the door.

Ettie opened the door to see Elsa-May's granddaughter with Elsa-May's great-granddaughter, Ivy, in front of her.

"Hello Becky, hello Ivy, Come in!" Ettie was amazed to see them, and by the look of the small bag it looked like Ivy might be staying for a while.

Becky said, "I didn't check with *Mammi*, but Ivy said she asked Ivy to stay here tonight."

"Did you, Elsa-May?" Ettie spun around to look at her sister. It wasn't the best time to have a young girl in the house.

"Hello, you two." Elsa-May pushed herself up from the

chair, and Ivy ran up to her and hugged her while Elsa-May was still doing her best to hold onto Snowy.

"Is this your new dog, *Mammi?*"

Elsa-May laughed. "That's him."

"Can I play with him?"

"You can. As soon as your *mamm* leaves, I'll let him go, and you can play with him outside."

Becky said, "I brought a change of clothing for her. I know you don't have much room in the *haus* here. She said last time she was here she slept on the couch."

"We can always make room for Ivy," Ettie said. "Can you stay for a cup of tea, Becky?"

"*Nee,* I must go. I've got errands to run today. Shall I collect her the same time tomorrow."

"*Jah,* that'll be fine," Elsa-May said.

As soon as Ivy's mother left, Elsa-May let go of Snowy. "If you run outside, he'll follow," Elsa-May said to Ivy.

"Okay." Ivy ran outside, but Snowy stayed staring up at Elsa-May.

"Go on, Snowy. Go off and play."

Snowy looked over at Ivy, who was calling him and then looked at Elsa-May again. As soon as Elsa-May took a step toward the back door, Snowy ran to Ivy.

Elsa-May sat down, and said to Ettie, "I'm exhausted just looking at Ivy. She's got so much energy."

"I'm surprised you had her here with all the murder things going on. Didn't we decide not to have her here until it was all over?"

"I didn't say she could come, Ettie. You heard what I said to her. I think she told her *mudder* that I said she could come here."

"Was it Ivy or her *mudder?* Maybe Becky wanted a little time to herself to run her errands."

Ettie and Elsa-May laughed.

"We should ask Ivy some questions later. I don't want her to think she can get away with making up stories to her *mudder* that I said she could come here today."

"And if we think Becky wanted some time alone, we'll not say anything?" Ettie asked.

"That's right. I remember what it was like to want time alone when my *kinner* were small."

"Becky's only got one and Ivy would be no problem at all she's so well behaved."

Elsa-May winced. "She does have the tendency to talk a lot."

The back door flung open, and the handle cracked against the wall. *"Mammi* come and play with us."

Just then, a knock sounded on their front door, and Snowy barked and ran to the door ahead of everyone followed closely by Ivy.

"Who could it be, *Mammi?"* Ivy stared up at Elsa-May as she walked to the door.

"We'll have to open it to find out." Elsa-May opened the door to see Brandy.

"Oh, I'm not interrupting anything, am I?"

"Hello, Brandy. This is my great-granddaughter, Ivy."

Brandy was distracted by Snowy who was pawing at her, and then he scratched her leg. "Oh no, the dog again."

"Hello," Ivy said to Brandy.

Elsa-May leaned down and picked up Snowy. "I'm sorry about the dog. Ivy, this is Ms. Winnie."

"Hello, Ms. Winnie," Ivy said.

"Hello, Ivy."

"Is Ms. the same as Miss?" Ivy asked Elsa-May.

"It's a little different, but it can be used for the same purpose," Elsa-May mumbled. "Perhaps you should go and see if you can help Ettie in the kitchen, Ivy."

"Okay. I'll take Snowy with me."

"That would be a good idea," Elsa-May said, as Ivy took Snowy out of her arms.

When Ivy and the dog were gone, Brandy stepped through the door.

"Sorry about that, Brandy. I'm looking after Ivy overnight."

Brandy rolled her eyes. "Lucky you."

"Come through to the living room and sit down."

Ettie joined them. "Hello, Brandy."

Brandy said, "Did you know that they've got an Amish man in custody?"

"Yes, we know him, and we were talking with him yesterday," Ettie said.

"What has he said?" Brandy inquired.

"He said Margaret was alive after the open house; he saw her."

"Before the robbery, then? Because I heard that a man has come forward and said he robbed Margaret of her engagement ring, but he says that he wasn't the one who killed her."

"We're not certain," Ettie said, not wanting to give Brandy too much information. Ettie was certain that it was still a secret that Margaret was working undercover; they had to be careful what they said.

"You spoke with the Amish man?" Brandy asked.

"Yes, we did." Elsa-May nodded.

"Did he see anyone or anything that would help the police?"

Elsa-May said, "That's something we don't know."

Brandy looked displeased. "Well, he must've said *something* to you."

"All he said was he happened to go past the house and saw her leaving the open house…"

Ettie cut across Elsa-May, "She said 'hello' and that was that. He said 'hello' back and kept going."

"He didn't say anything else? Did he see anyone around?" Brandy asked.

"Not that he told us. Have you talked to Detective Kelly lately?"

"He's busy. He questioned me the other day, and I haven't heard from him since. I was sure he'd call me."

"Do you know something, Brandy? Was there someone else or something else to see?" Ettie asked.

"The murderer, of course. If the man who stole the ring didn't kill her, then who did?"

"We've no idea," Elsa-May said.

"You don't know anything at all?" Brandy asked.

"No, nothing. I'm sure you'll be one of the first people the detective tells when he finds the guilty person."

Brandy tilted her head to one side. "Why do you say that?"

"She was your intern," Ettie said.

"Yes, that's right. This whole thing has me jumpy." She stood up. "I better go and get some work done. That'll keep my mind from this whole dreadful thing."

"Good idea," Elsa-May said.

CHAPTER 23

THE NEXT MORNING, soon after Ivy was collected by her mother, Detective Crowley came to their door.

"We are getting a lot of visitors lately," Ettie said. "Come in."

From her chair, Elsa-May called out, "Ettie and I were wondering when we'd hear from you again. Did Kelly fill you in with everything that's been going on?"

Crowley sat down. "Yes. He told me he let you know that Margaret was working undercover."

"You knew that when you came to see us the other day?" Elsa-May asked.

"Yes. I knew Margaret very well. We worked closely together many times. When I was here, I couldn't mention that to you. There were many of us who wanted to go to her funeral, but of course, we couldn't. You do know that it's still secret information?"

"We do," Elsa-May said.

Ettie leaned forward. "Have there been any developments?"

"Kelly is grateful for the help you two have given him. I've let him know that he can trust both of you to find things out for him."

"Thank you, but that's not answering Ettie's question."

"He's looked into everyone close to Margaret, which is Brandy, Josh Tomson, Paisley, Norman, Norman's ex-wife ..."

"And?"

"We're drawing a blank. The phone records of everyone show nothing that we don't already know. Everyone seems to have alibis."

"Where does that leave things?" Elsa-May asked. "If we don't find something soon someone might very well get away with killing her."

"They won't get away with it," Ettie stated.

The detective raised his eyebrows. "You mean the great judgment day in the sky?"

"We all have to give an account for what we have done," Elsa-May said.

"I hope it doesn't come to that. It's not ideal to have an unconvicted killer roaming around. I personally followed up on the whereabouts of the ex-wife at the time, and she has a solid alibi—as does Paisley."

"Does that mean Josh is still under suspicion?" Elsa-May asked.

"We've got no DNA evidence linking him to the crime. The evidence is circumstantial, and that will not hold up in court. I doubt he'll be charged with her murder."

"So you have to wait until more evidence turns up?" Ettie asked.

Elsa-May added, "That cuts out the daughter, the mother... what about Cartwright himself?"

Crowley winced. "His alibi is not airtight, but if he paid a man to steal the ring, it makes little sense he'd pay another man to come along and kill her, or even do it himself. His DNA was found on her person, but he was her fiancé, so that's understandable."

Ettie nodded. "And convenient for him."

"So, if that rules out Cartwright, the ex-wife, and Paisley, who does that leave?"

"I'm afraid it leaves Brandy and Josh Tomson. Unless there's another party we're missing."

"Josh must have just missed the murderer by seconds," Elsa-May said.

Crowley rubbed his jaw. "Buggies don't travel that quickly and if—according to him—if she was just about to call in the robbery, he must have seen the car of the person who did it."

"Yes, that's right because there's no through road. If you go past my house you can't keep going; you have to turn around and go past it again."

"The problem is, he can't recall anything. Or *says* he can't recall anything," Crowley said.

"Did Kelly send you to ask us to speak to him again?" Ettie asked.

"I was hoping I wouldn't be that obvious," Crowley said.

"I do hope Kelly has released him. He's not still in jail, is he?"

"He's been released."

"We'll talk to him today," Ettie said.

"Would you like a cup of hot tea?" Elsa-May asked Crowley.

"Always," he said with a smile.

WHEN CROWLEY LEFT, Ettie and Elsa-May got ready to head to Josh's house.

"It's certainly quiet with Ivy gone," Ettie said. "Did you see how Brandy reacted to Ivy? She seemed to care less for children than she does dogs."

Elsa-May sat as she laced up her boots. "Young children can be quite annoying, but when they're your *kin* that's an entirely different thing."

Ettie slumped into her couch. "Maybe that's it, Elsa-May!"

"What's it?" Elsa-May finished tying her laces and looked across at Ettie.

"The family bonds are hard to break. Even though Margaret left the community, she still had that bond with Sarah, her *schweschder.*"

Elsa-May's eyebrows drew together. "And?"

"Don't you see?"

"Apparently not!"

"Maybe Sarah holds the clue to all this. She could very well know a vital piece of information we've all missed," Ettie said.

"She talked to Kelly, and he didn't come up with anything."

"Remember what he told us about judgment being clouded by an expectation that someone is or isn't guilty."

"Jah, when we were talking about Josh, he said our judgment is clouded by us thinking he's innocent," Elsa-May said.

"Exactly, so when Kelly was talking to her, he wouldn't have expected her to know anything."

"I don't know what point you're trying to make, but if you think it will be any use we could talk with her before we go to see Josh."

"Let's do it," Ettie said with a nod.

CHAPTER 24

ELSA-MAY AND ETTIE got out of the taxi and hurried to Sarah's door.

They knocked, and one of Sarah's young boys answered the door. Before anyone spoke, Sarah appeared at the door behind him.

"Hello, come inside," Sarah said. "Come through to the kitchen." Sarah gave her little ones something to occupy them in the living room and then she joined them at the kitchen table.

"Looks like you're busy. Why don't you stay seated while I put a pot of tea on?" Elsa-May asked.

"That would be lovely. I never have anyone do anything for me anymore."

"That's the life of a *mudder*," Ettie said while Elsa-May stood and walked over to put the pot on to boil.

"What's happening? Have there been any developments?" Sarah asked.

"*Nee.* We just came over here to see how you are doing," Ettie said.

"I'm okay. I'm coping the best I can."

"We're certain that you were the only person that Margaret could trust completely. What did she tell you in that last visit?" Elsa-May asked.

Sarah nibbled on a fingernail and looked down.

Ettie spoke quietly. "We need to know, Sarah. You could be the one holding the key to finding her murderer."

"And we know she's gone, but you wouldn't want the same person who murdered her to murder again, would you?" Elsa-May asked.

"Nee. Nee, of course, I wouldn't. All right." Sarah heaved a big sigh. "We met a week before she was killed. She said she thought Norman found out that she was working undercover, but she wasn't certain."

"How?"

"They were in a restaurant and when she got up to go to the ladies' room someone she'd met on one of her other assignments saw her and called her by a different name. She wasn't certain Norman had heard what was said, but when she got back to the table, she noticed a change in his behavior." Sarah wiped her eyes. "I urged her to tell the police, but she said she didn't want to be extracted from the investigation. She said it would ruin her record. Instead of ruining her record, it ruined her life—she was killed."

"Thank you, Sarah. You've been a big help. Can we use the phone in your barn?" Ettie asked as she stood.

"Are you going to tell the police?"

"We have to," Elsa-May said.

Sarah nodded. "Okay."

In the barn, Ettie dialed the detective's mobile number and reached him on the first try.

"Detective Kelly, Sarah, Margaret's sister, just told us that Margaret thought that Norman had grown suspicious of her. Someone from a previous assignment recognized her and called her a different name and she thought Norman might have overheard."

"She didn't make that known to us," Kelly grumbled. "Did she say when that took place exactly?"

"The last visit, which was a week before she was killed."

"Interesting because according to Broadfoot, the robbery was arranged two weeks before her death."

"Norman wouldn't have known where she would've been because Brandy only arranged for her to be at the open house a day before," Ettie said.

"Good work, Mrs. Smith. I'll handle things from here. I'll contact Sarah to come in, so we can amend her statement."

ETTIE AND ELSA-MAY left Sarah and went on to Josh's house. They knocked on his door, and he answered looking as though he'd just got out of bed.

"Are you unwell?" Elsa-May asked.

"I'm feeling dreadful." He stepped back to let them in. They followed him to his living room. As soon as they sat, he said, "I've lied to the police."

"What about?" Ettie asked.

"I don't want to go to jail."

"What did you lie about, Josh?"

He rubbed his face in both of his hands. "When I got to your house, Ettie, I saw her car there and got out of my buggy. I knew no one would see us together because there was no one about. All I was hoping for was a quiet word with her."

The sisters waited patiently for him to continue.

When he finally spoke, he said, "I saw her lying there. I knew she was dead, and I panicked and drove away."

"Did you see anyone?" Ettie asked.

"I saw a man and a woman in a dark colored car when I was driving toward your *haus,* Ettie, and they'd just come from your *haus.*"

"Why didn't come forward about this sooner?"

"I was going to tell the police, but then that man said he saw me. I never saw that man, so I don't know how he saw me. I just had to make something up about her being alive so they wouldn't think I killed her."

"Josh, you've made things worse. Why couldn't you have just told Detective Kelly exactly what happened?" Elsa-May asked.

He shrugged. "I've never been good at talking. I'd never be able to go to a court or anything to defend myself. I'd freeze."

"They have lawyers to do that for you, Josh," Ettie said.

He raised his eyebrows. "I don't know how it works."

"Well, you're coming with us right now to tell Detective Kelly the truth of everything."

"I don't feel well."

"You'll feel much better once you tell the truth," Elsa-May said with a nod of her head.

"I can't spend another night in that cell, and I can tell that they think I killed her. What should I do?"

"Are you sure you didn't see a man driving away. He's made a statement that he passed you."

He shook his head. "*Nee,* Ettie, I saw a man and a woman in a dark car, and I'm certain they were heading away from your *haus.* I only remember them because I saw an open house sign and thought I'd go and have a look and assumed they must have just been at the open house. I didn't even know that Margaret would be there."

Ettie recalled that they had seen no open house signs when they had approached the house. "Could you identify the people in the car?"

"*Nee,* I didn't have a good look at them; I only got a glimpse."

"What about the car?" Elsa-May asked.

"Mercedes, large and dark blue. I remember that because it was odd to see a car like that around here."

"Would you feel better if the detective came here?"

"*Jah,* and can you both stay with me?"

Ettie nodded. "You've got a phone in the barn, haven't you?"

"*Jah* right by the door on the left."

"I'll call the detective and have him come here, but I'm certain he'll want you to record your statement."

"I'm unwell. Maybe we should do this tomorrow."

Ettie knew they had to move on things quickly. "I'll go and phone the detective while Elsa-May stays with you."

～

OVER THE PHONE in Josh's barn, Detective Kelly said, "Well, Mrs. Smith, I don't see how the time line fits. But that is the description of one of Cartwright's cars."

"Can you come and speak with him here? Maybe take a recording here? He's very distressed."

"I'll be there soon, Mrs. Smith. I'll bring a team with me, and we'll do our best to accommodate him—only for you, Mrs. Smith."

"Thank you, Detective." When Ettie hung up the phone, she sat on a bale of hay in the barn.

One scenario was that Cartwright murdered Margaret and saw Josh, so he paid someone to say that he'd robbed Margaret of the ring and had Broadfoot describe an Amish man as coming toward the house to make it look like Josh killed Margaret.

Why would Cartwright drive his own car if he intended to kill Margaret? Perhaps it just happened, and it wasn't premeditated. He could've confronted her with his suspicions of her being an undercover police officer.

"What if she admitted to it? *Nee,* she'd never do that and endanger her own life and all the hard work she'd put into investigating him," Ettie said out loud.

Ettie heard a meow and turned around. It was an orange tabby cat.

"Well, hello," Ettie said. "What do you think of the whole thing? And who was the man and who was the woman? The man could've been Cartwright, but who was the woman? It could've been one of his staff members; it could've been anyone."

Ettie remembered that the ex-wife of Cartwright and his daughter had rock solid alibis, but what about

Brandy? She couldn't recall whether the detective said anything about Brandy's alibi, or whether she had one at all.

The detective had seemed concerned about Brandy's change of name once they mentioned it in passing, but he never mentioned it again. Ettie couldn't decide what she thought about the whole thing; she still couldn't put all the pieces together, so she said goodbye to the cat and wandered back to the house to wait for Detective Kelly. Just as she was about to go inside, she turned around when a sudden thought occurred to her.

Detective Crowley! He can look into Brandy's past for me and see if there's anything there. She knew his number by heart, so she walked back into the barn, picked up the phone, and then dialed his number.

"Hello," Crowley answered.

"Oh, you're there."

"Yes."

"That's good."

"Ettie? Is that you?"

"Yes, it's me."

"What can I do for you?"

Ettie did her best to gather her thoughts.

"Hello? Ettie, are you still there?"

"I'm still here; I'm thinking. I'm wondering if you might be able to look up someone's past for me."

"Who?"

"Brandy Winnie."

"The realtor?"

"Yes. She told me some time ago when I first met her that she changed her name so it would fit better on her business card. I got to thinking that maybe there's another reason she changed her name."

"She's well known. It's doubtful she's hiding anything. Do you mean you want me to find out if she's got a criminal record?"

"Yes, that kind of thing."

"Ettie, she can't have one. If she had a record, she wouldn't be able to be a realtor. They're very strict about that kind of thing."

"What if she was convicted under her old name and that's why she changed it?"

"I see what you mean. When did she change it?"

"I don't know exactly, but it was when she began her real estate career, I believe."

"Okay, give me her old name and I'll see what turns up."

"Really? You'd do that?"

The detective chuckled. "I can't play golf all year round. It won't hurt to keep my hand in, just in case I take up that new career I was telling you about."

"Thank you. I'd appreciate that." Ettie gave him Brandy's former name, and then promptly hung up the phone before she hurried back to the house.

When she entered the kitchen, she found Josh was sitting down at the table having a cup of hot tea with Elsa-May.

"Would you like a cup, Ettie?"

"Jah."

It was a good half-hour wait before Detective Kelly arrived with a few officers. Ettie and Elsa-May stayed in the kitchen while Josh was interviewed in the living room.

"Poor Josh," Elsa-May whispered. "To find Margaret dead and have to lie about it through fear of being accused of her death."

"That would've been a burden too heavy for him to bear."

"I do hope they don't find a reason to lock him up again."

"If they do, we'll call Bishop John. He'll be the best person for Josh to pray with so he can get through this time," Ettie said.

"What do you make of it all? Nothing seems to make sense."

"When I was in the barn I called Crowley. I asked him to see what he could find out about Brandy Winnie. I thought what if Brandy was the woman in the car?"

"Do you think so?"

Ettie hunched her shoulders. "As you said, so far nothing makes sense, so we know that there's information missing somewhere."

"It'll be interesting to see what he turns up. I always thought there was something strange about the woman."

"She might have changed her name all those years ago for a reason."

"Do you remember when she was telling us her name when we first met her?" Elsa-May asked.

"I do. I recall that she readily told us her last name, but was more hesitant to tell us her first. Now, that could've been that she was embarrassed to have such a dreadful name, or was she protecting her true identity?" Ettie.

"And then she possibly thought, *What harm will it do to tell these two old Amish ladies my real name?*"

"I got chills down my back when you just said that, Elsa-May."

"If she was involved in murder, what motivation did she have?"

"Love. Didn't Crowley tell us a long time ago that most murders are committed over love, revenge, or money?" Ettie asked.

"Brandy's love for Cartwright?"

Ettie nodded. "And she would've been set for life if she married him and would never have had to work another day in her life. So you could also say it was money motivated."

As they each finished a second cup of tea, Kelly came into the kitchen. "Thank you, both of you. His testimony has been invaluable. We'll go back and question Broadfoot. It seems he lied to us, and either he knows who killed Margaret or he did it himself."

"Who do you think the man and the woman were in the car?" Elsa-May asked.

"Brandy perhaps?" Ettie suggested.

"No, Mrs. Smith. There's nothing to implicate Brandy Winnie."

Ettie stared at the detective. "She's got an alibi, then?"

He nodded and then said, "I've got to drive the men back to the station so we can get a statement prepared for Josh to sign. We've explained to Josh that an officer will be back with the document for signing later today. I'm organizing a warrant for Cartwright's car. Broadfoot says he stole a car, but no car matching the description he gave us has ever been reported as missing. And it's never been seen where he reportedly abandoned it."

"You believe what Josh said?" Elsa-May asked.

"As much as I believe anyone's testimony. It'll be interesting to hear what Broadfoot will have to say once he hears what Josh has said."

CHAPTER 25

WHEN ELSA-MAY and Ettie got home, they were still bothered by everything.

"Not now, Snowy. I'll walk you later. I need a rest." Snowy stopped trying to jump up on Elsa-May as she sat on her usual chair. He went to his bed in the corner and made himself comfortable.

"It'll be just Broadfoot's word against Josh's. So it seems that Broadfoot was the one driving the dark blue car, and he had a female passenger," Elsa-May said.

Ettie untied the strings of her prayer *kapp*. "I was wondering if it was Cartwright driving the car and he paid someone—Broadfoot, to come forward and say he stole the diamond, and she was alive when he left. That way, he could implicate Josh and make it look like Josh was the one who killed her."

"That does make sense, Ettie. And if that's right, the only thing we don't know now is who the woman was and exactly who the man was driving the car. Didn't Josh say that Margaret always insisted on wearing the fake ring?"

"Jah, he said that. What does that have to do with anything?"

"Why was her finger all swollen like that as though someone was pulling it off her finger?" Elsa-May asked.

"I guess the insurance company would need to believe that the ring was stolen. Once it was on the autopsy report that there was evidence of the ring being forcibly taken, that would strengthen Cartwright's claim."

Elsa-May nodded.

Ettie stretched her arms over her head. "Hopefully, Kelly will sort it all out, and I'm glad he believed what Josh said."

"Josh always avoided telling us the truth, and now we know why. Seeing her dead, lying there like that must have scared him especially after she told him all those things about the people she'd been investigating."

"He could've thought he might be next," Ettie said.

"Seems like whoever killed her knew that Josh didn't get a good look at them."

THE NEXT MORNING just after they'd finished their breakfast, Crowley knocked on Elsa-May and Ettie's door.

"I hope I'm not too early?" he asked as he stepped through the door.

"No. Come in. What is the time?" Ettie asked.

"It's half past nine," he answered.

"We're just having a cup of tea. Would you like one?" Elsa-May asked.

"No. I won't even sit down. I've just stopped by to let you know that I found something on Boadicea."

"What is it?" Ettie asked.

"She was once charged with murder."

Ettie gasped.

"The charges were then downgraded to conspiracy to commit murder and then the charges were dropped altogether."

"Does Kelly know?" Elsa-May asked.

"I called him late in the evening yesterday, but he already knew. He didn't seem to think it warranted looking into her further."

"Why not?" Ettie frowned.

Crowley spread his arms out. "He seems to have some affection for her. There's not much more I can do; it's his investigation, not mine."

"That's just not right," Elsa-May said. "Ettie, we need to pay Detective Kelly a visit."

"No, Elsa-May. You can't tell him how to do his job. How do we know he doesn't know other things he's not letting us in on. He's done that plenty of times before."

Crowley chuckled.

"Do you know anything else? Did Kelly tell you something and tell you to keep it quiet?" Ettie asked.

"If he did, I wouldn't be able to tell you, now, would I? You think Brandy's guilty?" Crowley asked.

"She's been accused of being involved with murder before, so what would you think?" Ettie asked.

"I'd take a closer look at her whereabouts at the time

of the murder," Crowley said before he sighed. "I am going past the station if you would like me to drive you."

"Thank you."

"We're ready now," Elsa-May snarled. "And I'll have a few words to say."

"I'd tread carefully, Elsa-May. You don't know what Kelly's got up his sleeve. He's a good operator, one of the best," Crowley said.

"Maybe you should calm down a little," Ettie said to Elsa-May. "Why don't we leave it until this afternoon and then if you still feel as strongly we'll go and see him then?"

Elsa-May nodded. "I suppose you're both right. I'll calm down and think things through before I say anything to him, but I'm certain he's letting his attraction to Brandy get in his way of seeing her as a proper suspect."

"Is that a 'no' to the drive to the station?" Crowley asked.

"Yes, that's a 'no.' Thank you for the offer. If you hear anything else, do you think you could let us know?" Ettie asked.

"I will, but I'm unlikely to hear anything on the golf course."

"Is that why you're dressed like that?" Ettie looked him up and down. She'd never seen him in anything but a suit. He certainly looked odd in the geometric patterned shorts, the two-tone shoes, and the short-sleeved t-shirt.

"That's right. This is what we have to wear on the course. They have a strict dress code."

When the detective left, Elsa-May took Snowy for a walk to try to calm down.

LATER THAT DAY, the detective didn't look pleased to see the two sisters at the waiting room of the police station. He showed them into his office and told them about Cartwright's car.

"We showed Josh the impounded car belonging to Cartwright. Josh said it was the same model as the one he saw heading away from the house."

"Have you spoken to Brandy again?" Ettie asked Kelly.

"About what?"

Elsa-May said, "About the fact that she came up on murder charges some years ago."

The detective glowered. "How did you find out? She was never convicted, and there's no record."

Elsa-May held her chin high. "We have ways."

"Keep it to yourselves. We're moving forward on trying to get a confession," Kelly said.

"A confession from whom?" Ettie asked.

"Go home!" Kelly snapped. "I'll personally come by your home and let you know when something breaks. It's not far away."

Elsa-May tipped her head to one side as she studied Kelly's face. "You know something, then?"

"I'm not prepared to say more, but both of you being here sticking your noses in could possibly jeopardize everything."

Ettie stood. "Come on, Elsa-May."

"I'm coming. I can't get up as fast as you."

When they were outside the station, Elsa-May groaned. "That man's annoying."

"Most men are."

Elsa-May sniggered. "Very true."

"Let's go and find that cake shop again."

"You need another treat?"

Ettie nodded. "I do."

"You'll be my size soon if you keep eating so many cakes."

"I can't seem to put on weight. Anyway, if I do, I'll cut down on my sweets."

"I'll come and watch you eat. I don't want to be doing all that walking with Snowy to spoil it with cake every day. I could do with another cup of tea."

While Ettie and Elsa-May were walking up the road to the café where they'd found the delicious cakes, they saw Brandy walking toward them.

She took off her sunglasses and stopped still as they approached. After they had greeted Brandy, she asked where they were going.

Ettie pointed to the café. "We went into that café a few days ago and discovered they've got a delightful array of cakes. That's where we're going."

"Yes, I know. I've been in there before."

"We're going to sit down and give ourselves a treat," Ettie said.

"That sounds like exactly what I need after a hard day. Mind if I join you?" Brandy asked.

"Please do," Elsa-May said.

When they'd made their selections they all sat around a small table.

"Were you coming from the police station?" Brandy asked.

Elsa-May nodded. "Yes, we were."

"Have there been any developments?"

"They have taken Norman Cartwright's car. They've impounded it, but I suppose you'd already know that." Ettie stared at Brandy.

"No. How would I know that?" Brandy's body stiffened, and her face turned ghastly pale.

"We thought you were a friend of his," Ettie said.

"I know him. That's all. I'm not a friend. I'm not a friend, at all. A friend would tell someone if they had their car impounded. What were they hoping to find?"

Elsa-May added, "Kelly tells us he's pretty close to finding the murderer. He appears to have it all figured out."

"What else did he say?"

"He didn't say too much exactly, but from what he did say, he had it all figured out. Maybe a witness to the whole thing has come forward," Ettie said.

Brandy frowned. "Where would they have found a witness? There are no close neighbors to your house, Ettie."

Ettie gave a quick shrug of her shoulders. "I'm not certain. We've always got birdwatchers coming here at this time of year; maybe one of them saw something through their binoculars."

"Let's hope so," Brandy said just as the waitress brought their cakes to the table.

"The tea won't be a moment," the waitress said.

Ettie noticed that Brandy's hands were trembling as she picked up the fork to eat her cake.

"Are you not feeling well, Brandy?" Elsa-May asked.

"I've had a bad day that's all. Why? Do I look sick?"

"You do look a little pale, and your hands are shaking."

She clasped both hands together and smiled. "I've not eaten today that's why. I've got low blood sugar."

"The cake will fix that," Ettie said as she broke off a piece of ginger cake.

Brandy forced a smile and took a small bite of her chocolate mini-cupcake.

The waitress brought their tea.

"Ah, a nice cup of tea," said Elsa-May. "Not as good as cake, but I'll have to be grateful for it anyway."

"So, you don't know why the police took Norman's car?" Brandy asked.

"Looking for evidence I suppose. I can't think of any other reason they'd take it," Ettie said.

"I've traveled in his car before. I think I also had some of my open house signs in his car. I suppose you think that's odd, but he collected them from person who makes the signs for me. We are business acquaintances, so my prints would've been in his car."

"Yes, you seemed to know him well. That's what Ettie and I thought at Margaret's funeral since you were sitting next to him and traveling in the car with him."

"Brandy, correct me if I'm wrong, but I think that you're in love with Norman Cartwright, and you killed for him," Ettie said.

Brandy sat stunned into silence.

Ettie cleared her throat. "You gave Margaret some of your medication, enough to make her drowsy and feel unwell, then you sent her to my open house. Meanwhile, you visited Norman and told him that Margaret was visiting her old Amish boyfriend behind his back and was possibly having an affair. Norman became enraged and had to confront her at once. You told him where she was and offered to show him the exact house where she'd be."

Ettie took a deep breath. "By this time, everyone had left the open house, and Margaret was packing up. An argument followed, and you looked on as Norman pulled the ring from her finger. You slipped something around her neck and pulled hard. Margaret died quickly since she'd already had trouble breathing due to the drugs you gave her without her knowledge—the drugs that were prescribed for you. She was strangled by someone tall, and you're tall."

"Ettie, I didn't know you thought so badly of me." She glanced over at Elsa-May and then looked back at Ettie. "None of what you said is true, but I've covered up the truth to protect someone else."

"What is it, Brandy?" Elsa-May leaned forward.

"I've kept quiet about information I have on someone," Brandy repeated.

Elsa-May stared at Brandy. "You know who killed Margaret?"

Brandy nodded as tears welled in her eyes. "I hate to even hear myself say it, but I do."

"You should go and tell Detective Kelly now," Ettie said while Brandy sobbed into her cupped hands. Ettie passed her some paper napkins.

"I'll lose everything I've built up. If I get charged for …"

"For what?" Elsa-May asked.

"For anything. If I'm charged for anything I'll have to find other work and real estate is what I was born to do."

"Maybe it won't come to that," Ettie said. "But if you know something you must tell."

"You're such an intelligent and vibrant woman, you'd be able to do anything," Elsa-May said. "Don't limit yourself."

She sniffed. "Do you really think so?"

"Yes. Now if you know anything, it's better that you go and tell the detective before he finds out and comes looking for you," Elsa-May said. "He's not far away from the truth."

"That's right, isn't it? It's better if I go and tell them first."

Ettie nodded, quite unsure of what Brandy knew and not sure she should ask.

"Do you me to walk there with you?"

"I'll go there by myself. Thank you for the offer, and something tells me I should go now." Brandy reached into her purse and flipped her compact open. "I look dreadful." She dabbed some concealer under her eyes and reapplied her lipstick.

"There, good as new," Elsa-May said with a smile.

"I'll go now." Brandy stood and hurried out of the café.

Ettie leaned over, and whispered to Elsa-May, "What if she's not going to the station? She could be getting on the next plane."

"From what she said, she seems to know what really happened and wasn't directly involved."

"Like the last time she was arrested?" Ettie asked.

"Seems so. Ettie, don't you think I deserve a treat after that?"

Ettie laughed. "You certainly do. I won't stop you from having a cake."

"Actually, all I want to do now is go home."

"Me too."

CHAPTER 26

Elsa-May and Ettie spent the rest of the evening wondering what Brandy had told the police. It wasn't until the afternoon of the following day that they got a visit from Detective Kelly. Ettie had been baking all day and heard a car pull up outside the house. She looked out the kitchen window to see Kelly getting out of his car.

"Elsa-May, put Snowy outside, Detective Kelly's coming to the door."

By the time he got to the door Ettie and Elsa-May were standing there with the door open, waiting for him.

He looked up at them with a big smile before he walked up the steps of their porch.

"You look like you have something to tell us, Detective," Elsa-May said.

"And both of you look like you want to hear something." He laughed. "I do have a lot to tell you."

"Come inside and make yourself comfortable," Ettie said.

"I'll come in and sit down," he said. "Unless you fixed those chairs I won't be making myself comfortable."

"See, what did I say?" Ettie said to Elsa-May.

"We're getting them fixed soon," Elsa-May assured Detective Kelly.

Once they were seated, he began, "I believe you were speaking to Brandy yesterday afternoon after I told you not to."

"Is that what she said?" Elsa-May asked.

He shook his head. "It doesn't matter now. She said she had been talking to you …"

"We ran into her after we left your office; it was purely coincidental," Ettie assured him.

"I didn't know you ladies would believe in coincidences."

Elsa-May and Ettie stared at each other and then looked back at the detective.

"After she spoke to you, she came and told me what happened on the day Margaret was murdered. She was with Cartwright, who had expressed disappointment with Margaret. He said he wanted to speak to her immediately, and Brandy told him she was finishing up at the open house."

"What was she doing with him?" Ettie asked.

"Does it matter?" Kelly asked frowning.

"It might," Elsa-May added.

"Ladies! Let me finish!"

A hush fell across the room.

"Do you want me to tell you what happened or not?" he asked.

"Please continue, Detective; Ettie will keep quiet."

Ettie glared at her sister, but what could she say? The detective would only get angrier if she pointed out to Elsa-May that she was also guilty of speaking.

"Thank you," Kelly said, "Now, I've lost where I was up to."

Elsa-May said, "You were up to the part where Brandy just happened to be with Cartwright even though she couldn't personally attend Ettie's open house."

"That's right, thank you. And, Cartwright expressed his disappointment in Margaret and had to confront her about something. Brandy went with him in the car to show him where the open house was being held, and an argument broke out between the two of them—Margaret and Cartwright. He said he was breaking off the engagement and wanted his ring back. He pulled it off her finger, and then she said she would go public with all his secret dealings. In a fit of rage, he strangled her."

"That's it?" Ettie asked in disgust.

The detective drew his mouth in tightly. "What do you mean? You're probably thinking it doesn't make sense if she were wearing the fake ring, but he could've pulled the fake one off as a symbolic gesture."

"She stood by and watched the man strangle her intern without lifting a finger or calling for help?" Ettie asked.

"Where would he find something to strangle her with?" Elsa-May asked. "I would've thought strangling would've been a pre-meditated thing. Did he bring a rope or something with him?"

The detective lifted both hands to silence them. "Poor Brandy stood by and watched in horror as it all unfolded.

She was too much in shock to take in too many details, according to her," Kelly said.

"Sounds to me like she was in it with him. That's the only thing that makes sense because why come clean about the whole thing now?" Ettie said.

The detective stared at Ettie. "Brandy was scared of the man. He's a very powerful man. They've got a long history together, and he was convinced that he could trust Brandy with the secret."

"What did Cartwright say about what Brandy says?" Elsa-May asked.

He lifted a finger in the air. "Ahh. I just told you Brandy's story; now *his* story is different. Cartwright says that he and Brandy were dating on and off before he fell in love with Margaret. He didn't know how jealous Brandy was of Margaret until he asked Brandy to take Margaret under her wing as her intern. The day of the murder Brandy told him that Margaret had been secretly seeing an old boyfriend, and he went to confront her about it. He admits to pulling the ring from her in anger, and she dropped crying to her knees holding her hand. He says Brandy came up behind her and slipped something around her neck. It was all over fast. He slapped Brandy across her face because he never meant for Margaret to die."

Ettie covered her mouth in shock.

"Who do you believe?" Elsa-May asked the detective.

"There's more!" he said.

Elsa-May inched herself forward on her chair. "What is it?"

"The toxicology report has come back showing that

Margaret had opioids in her system. She'd received a large dose."

"What's that?" Ettie asked.

"A type of drug. And Brandy has a prescription for the exact opioids; she uses them for pain management of her chronic arthritis. Margaret would've already had difficulty breathing by then, and that's why the strangulation would've been speedy."

"This falls in line with Cartwright saying that it was over quickly," Ettie commented. "So it was Brandy?"

"Yes, Brandy killed the woman known as Margo Rivers, and Cartwright tried to help her cover it up. Before she sent Margo to the open house, she would've given her something with the drug in it. Then she went to Cartwright and told him that Margo was still seeing her Amish ex-boyfriend. Once he was enraged by that knowledge, Brandy told him where Margo could be found and traveled with him."

The detective paused, and then began again, "She was most likely hoping that he would be enraged and do something to cause her death, and when he didn't, she'd come prepared. According to our experts, Margo would've had slurred speech, and her breathing would've been heavily affected. Hopefully, it was all over quickly, and she wasn't aware of what was happening."

"I'm glad this whole thing has been solved," Elsa-May said.

Ettie pushed her lips out into a pout. "You could've told us that as soon as you arrived."

The detective smirked. "I get so little amusement in

life. I like to see the looks on your faces as I tell you every detail."

Elsa-May sighed. "Poor Margaret. I wonder how her last moments were."

"That is something we'll never know," Kelly said.

"So, it's fairly obvious that the Broadfoot man was paid to say he'd stolen the ring and to say that Margaret was alive when he left her," Ettie stated.

"Yes, he admitted it when we confronted him with the truth. He was able to pick Josh out of a lineup because Cartwright had described him well. Broadfoot often did jobs for Cartwright. Although him coming forward like that implicated Cartwright for the insurance fraud, Cartwright's real aim was for it to clear him of the murder and keep attention from Brandy."

"That's what Ettie said about Broadfoot right away. She didn't believe him."

"It was just a thought," Ettie said. "A coincidental thought."

"So have they both been charged?" Elsa-May asked.

"Yes, Brandy has been charged with the murder of Margo Rivers. Margaret had her name legally changed, as you know. Along with his other charges, Cartwright has been charged with withholding information, assault, tax evasion, and perverting the course of justice."

"It's hard to imagine that Brandy could kill someone," Ettie said holding her hands together over her chest.

"It is indeed. She seemed a delightful woman. So it seems you need another realtor to sell your house, Ettie."

"That's the least of my worries."

"Josh is totally in the clear now?" Elsa-May inquired.

"One hundred percent."

"That's good to know. Thank you, Detective," Elsa-May said with a smile.

The detective leaned forward in the creaky chair. "Thank you both for your help in all of this."

"I don't know that we did anything," Ettie said.

"You did, you made my job much easier. Now, have you ladies run out of coffee?"

"Would you like a cup?"

"I'd love one," he said. "That's normally the first thing you ask me."

Elsa-May stood. "I'll fix us some coffee and cake. Ettie has just made a ginger cake."

"Yes, it's the first one I've made, and you can be the taste-tester. I don't know if I'll be able to eat anything; I'm so upset that Brandy could do something like that. I trusted her."

"I'm sorry it turned out the way it did, and the force was sad to see a good officer be cut down like she was. We're holding a proper memorial service for her in two weeks now that we don't have to hide that she was under-cover. All her co-workers can pay their respects. You can come too, and Elsa-May."

"Thank you, detective, but I think we've gone to too many funerals in our lives. We already paid our respects to Margaret. I suppose you'll inform Sarah, Margaret's sister and the rest of Margaret's family?"

"Yes, of course. We've got Margaret's badge and personal things."

"You might want to take them to Sarah's house. I don't know that her parents would want the badge as a reminder of the secrets she kept from them."

The detective nodded. "I'll do that."

Ettie wiped a tear from her eye.

"Are you all right, Mrs. Smith?"

"It's sad all around. Such a senseless waste of life, and for what?"

"When life doesn't turn out the way people planned, they often try to force the dice to fall in their favor," the detective said.

"By killing?" Ettie asked.

"They often see that as the answer to their problems. Brandy was certain that with her competition out of the way Norman Cartwright would fall in love with her. She might have even thought the murder would've bonded the two of them together."

Ettie shuddered. "That's a horrid thought."

Elsa-May brought a tray of coffee and cake into the room.

The detective sprang to his feet. "Let me help you with that." When he sat back down, he said, "I suppose it's thrilling for you ladies to see a real detective in action?"

"What do you mean?" Elsa-May asked.

"Watching me put the pieces together." He smiled as he tapped a finger on his head.

"You did well, Detective," Ettie said, as she poured him a cup of coffee from the pot.

When the detective left, Elsa-May let Snowy back in

the house. Snowy ran around sniffing everywhere the detective had been.

"That's right we had someone in the house," Elsa-May said to the dog.

"Oh, Elsa-May, why did Margaret go in for such a dangerous life?"

"She thought she was helping people, and she probably did help people during the years she was with the police force."

"And Brandy; who would've thought she would be capable of murder?"

"She did have drive and ambition," Elsa-May stated.

"I don't think the two go together—murder and ambition."

"They did in this particular case."

"I suppose you're right," Ettie murmured.

Elsa-May sat back down. "What? You're agreeing with me?"

"I am."

Snowy started barking and ran to the door seconds before a knock sounded. Both sisters pushed themselves to their feet and walked to the door. Before Ettie opened the door, Elsa-May scooped Snowy up.

At the doorstep stood Jeremiah and Ava.

"Look at you two," Ettie said. "You look so happy. Come in."

As Jeremiah walked past Elsa-May, he patted Snowy. "There's the culprit," he said.

"He's usually very good," Elsa-May said.

"*Jah,* he's usually good because he's chewing on my slippers or things he shouldn't be chewing on."

"Don't listen to Ettie." Elsa-May laughed.

They all sat in the living room, and Jeremiah rocked on the wooden chair. "This chair needs some serious attention."

"I've been meaning to ask you to take a look at these chairs."

"We should just get new ones and be done with it," Ettie said.

"*Nee!* I can fix these. I'll take a couple with me today and bring them back when I finish and then take the next two. They'll be as *gut* as new."

Elsa-May jutted out her bottom jaw. "See, Ettie, what did I say?"

"All right. You got your way again, Elsa-May!"

Elsa-May chuckled as she sat with Snowy in her arms. "I can tell you've got some news for us. Are you expecting, Ava?"

Ava gasped, and her face turned red. "*Nee,* but we've both come here because … you tell them, Jeremiah."

"We'd like to buy your *haus,* Ettie."

"You would?"

"We would. And that way my *grossmammi* can live with us in the *grossdaddi haus,*" Ava said.

"What about your new home that you built, Jeremiah?"

"We'll sell it," Ava answered for him.

"I've done so much work on your *haus,* Ettie. I know it pretty well, and we both like it. It's the place we got to know each other better."

Ava beamed a smile at Jeremiah, and then said to Ettie, "We can pay what Brandy originally said it was worth if that's okay with you."

Ettie laughed. "If that's what you want to do I'm more than happy to sell it to both of you. I don't want you to pay too much; we can talk about the price after you sell your other house."

"Would you wait for it to sell?" Jeremiah asked. "We'd need the money from the sale of it to pay you."

"*Jah.* I will. I think Agatha would love for Ava to live in her *haus.* That makes me so happy." Ettie wiped a tear from her eye hoping no one would see it.

Jeremiah and Ava looked lovingly into each other's eyes.

Ettie stood up. "I'll go and fix us some tea." Ettie managed to get to the kitchen before another tear fell. So many things had happened surrounding Agatha's old house, and now a lovely young couple would live there and one day, soon she hoped, they would raise their *kinner* there.

Once she'd put the pot on to boil, she sat at the kitchen table and held her head in her hands. Life was a cycle, some of it good and some bad. Long ago, Horace had been murdered in the house, and then hidden under the floorboards, Margaret had been murdered right in front of the house, but soon that same house would be filled with the love and laughter of two wonderful young people.

The thing is to hold in your mind only the good, Ettie reminded herself.

Finally, brethren, whatsoever things are true, whatsoever things are honest, whatsoever things are just, whatsoever things are pure, whatsoever things are lovely, whatsoever things are of

*good report; if there be any virtue, and if there be any praise,
think on these things.*
Philippians 4:8

Thank you for your interest in
Amish Murder Too Close.

The next book in the series is:
Amish Quilt Shop Mystery

There's a dead man in her quilt store!

Now someone is trying to kill her.

Bethany has finally realized her dream of opening her own business, but that dream turns into a nightmare when she finds a dead body in her store.

Ettie Smith can't stay away when there's a mystery to solve.

When Ettie uncovers some startling information, she realizes Bethany's life is in danger and warns her to trust no one.

Is the murderer someone close to them? Can Ettie find out before it's too late?

For a full list of Samantha Price's books visit:
www.SamanthaPriceAuthor.com

ABOUT SAMANTHA PRICE

Samantha Price wrote stories from a young age, but it wasn't until later in life that she took up writing full time. Formally an artist, she exchanged her paintbrush for the computer and, many best-selling book series later, has never looked back.

Samantha is happiest on her computer lost in the world of her characters.

She is best known for the Ettie Smith Amish Mysteries series and the Expectant Amish Widows series.

To learn more about Samantha Price and her books visit:

www.samanthapriceauthor.com

Samantha Price loves to hear from her readers. Connect with her at:

samanthaprice333@gmail.com
www.facebook.com/SamanthaPriceAuthor
Follow Samantha Price on BookBub
Twitter @ AmishRomance

CPSIA information can be obtained
at www.ICGtesting.com
Printed in the USA
LVHW050727280420
654657LV00010B/1589